FROM BEST SELLING AUTHOR

SUSAN HARRIS

I0640091

Own The Night

A MURDERING HOUR NOVEL

OWN THE NIGHT
Copyright ©2024 Susan Harris
All rights reserved.

ISBN: **978-1-63422-553-3** (paperback)
ISBN: **978-1-63422-543-4** (e-book)
Cover Design by: Gem Promotions
Typography by: Gem Promotions
Proofing by: Ashley Brilinski

Listen to them, the children of the night.
What music they make!

- BRAM STOKER

DRACULA

MAX

There was something about the night that Max found comforting, like the mask of goodness the day brought was stripped away, revealing the murkiness of how the world truly was. In the dark of night, the shadows revealed the evil that stalked through the city streets. There was a reason why Max had a penchant for calling midnight the murdering hour.

Inclining his head toward the Garda who was standing at the mouth of the alleyway, as a barrage of forensic investigators were trying to gather as much evidence as possible in the piss drenched laneway. Max angled his body to the side to allow one of the techs to take a bag of evidence toward the waiting vans.

Taking a moment to roam his eyes over the scene, Max tried to filter out all of the busyness and focus on his surroundings. This part of Cork City had recently been rejuvenated by investment, with swanky restaurants and bars opening up and offering employment, but a place for the more well off Corkonians to splash the cash. Grand Parade and the surrounding area had become the hub of the rich, but that brought with it a hell of a lot more trouble than the city ever had before.

The alleyway, called Tobin Street, was situated between two bars, with two very different clientele. The Player's Lounge was a members only sort of establishment where only the most elite could get through the doors. Max had never ventured inside despite his curiosity, but then he wasn't known to be the partying kind of guy.

The Player's Lounge occupied the building that used to be home to Singers Corner, a staple of Cork City, however even from the outside, it looked nothing like it had back when Max was growing up. It had been given a glow up, that's what his sister had said to him once when they drove passed. Sleek black that almost blended impeccably with the night, tinted windows that screamed exclusivity and privacy. The only thing of note on the building was a little plaque next to the main double doors, also black, that had The Player's Lounge etched into it.

"Max, come here a sec!"

Max paused his surveyal of the crime scene and headed toward the voice that had called his name with a familiarity that very few had. Rían Kelly was crouched over the body, wearing one of those white suits, complete with matching boots and gloves. The only thing Max's oldest friend did that was outside of policy was to not bother with the hood, because it would mess up his already intentionally styled messy looking blond locks.

Rían and Max had both attended the same private boarding school on the Cork and Kerry border, had been roommates because the school didn't believe in isolating students with single dorm rooms. Rían had been popular and outgoing, with an easy charm and a smile that seemed to draw people to him like a moth to a flame.

Max, however, had what his sister Shauna liked to call a resting bitch face.

Max glanced down at the young woman who had been the victim of a heinous crime, and memorized the details. Her hair was Irish red, or more accurately ginger but the dark roots indicated that it was a bad dye job and not natural. Her pale skin looked a ghostly white against the dark crimson that was caked into her temple and her hair.

Her face was littered with bluish-purple discoloration marks on her skin, meaning she'd been beaten before her death. Max could almost be certain that when Rían finished his autopsy, that she'd have broken bones in her face, among other things. The way her skirt was pulled up around her waist and her knickers were around her ankles, Max was certain he was looking at something more than a murder.

Rían lifted the dead woman's hand, taking a swab as he

sighed. "Good girl, put up a fight didn't ya. Got me some nice DNA under your fingernails to catch the fucking bastard."

See that was why Rían was more likable than he was...he even tried to charm the dead.

Max heard some shuffling behind him, turned his gaze toward the uniformed officer that was lingering at the fringes, holding a handbag that Max assumed belonged to the slain woman. She shifted on her feet and Max could almost smell the nervousness dripping from her pores. He might not know who she is, but it was obvious that the fresh meat Garda knew all about him.

"Did you find an ID?"

"Yes sir," The Garda managed to splutter out. "I mean, Detective Sergeant De Barra."

Max huffed out an exasperated breath as he heard the sound of Rían's chuckle. "Sir is grand, Garda. The girl's name?"

"Molly McBride, sir. According to her driver's license Molly is twenty-four years old. She's a hostess in the Player's Lounge." The female Garda's eyes widened, then she stumbled over her words and for a minute, Max thought the panic would swallow her up. "I mean she was a hostess...cause she's dead."

There was a sharp intake of breath from the Garda and Max knew that the girl was on the cusp of either jacking it all in and saying fuck it or puking all over his crime scene.

"How 'bout you take that over to the crime techs for logging into evidence? Then see if your Sergeant needs help with taking witness statements."

The Garda nodded and hurried off. Max felt the weight of Rían's gaze on him. Glancing downward, as Rían rolled his eyes and Max arched a brow. "What?"

"You enjoy scaring the newbies, don't you?"

"A little fear will do them good. And she was about to vomit on my crime scene."

Rían shook his head aback to examining the body. "You would think that after all the years spent being my best friend, some of my irresistible charm would rub off on you."

Max snorted as he crouched down, making sure to stay out of

Rían's way and light, though that was sparse enough as they had yet to set up any lighting as Rían preferred to work that way.

"I don't like people. So, no fucking need to be charming, Rían. That's what I have you for."

That drew another little chuckle from Rían, and Max heard him mutter that it was funny how they had ended up in the jobs they did; Rían with all his charm tended to the dead, and Max, who hated to be around people, dealt with them more frequently than Rían did.

But then again, there was a reason why Max had requested to work the night shift on a permanent basis. And it was why he never worked with a partner no matter how many times his Chief Superintendent tried to convince him that he needed one. His solving rate was the highest in his station, hell in all of Cork, so he had some leeway with demands.

Rían's parents were both doctors, his dad was a top Obstetrics and fertility doctor, and his mam was a neurosurgeon who hospitals all around the world flew her out to perform the most complex of surgeries. When Rían had gone to medical school, his family name had been a curse and Rían had felt smothered by it. So, he'd decided to say hell to it all and decided to become a forensic pathologist. He was the youngest in the entire island of Ireland.

Max's parents were old money, but his mam used to deal in antiquities, and his dad had been an architect. Max had loved to sit and watch his dad work, constructing model buildings in his office for clients. There was many a time Max had sat at the other side of the table, trying to mirror his dad's work with his own Lego.

That seemed like a fucking lifetime ago.

Now, his dad was long since dead, his ashes scattered in the wind, and his mam, she had been a permanent resident of the Brookhaven Residential Care Home since the day she murdered his dad ten years ago. Max had been sixteen at the time when he had walked into the house one night at midnight, after leaving a party early during half term, to the sound of ten-year-old Shauna's cries from her locked bedroom, and the sight of his mam pulling the leg of a chair from his dad's chest.

In the midst of what doctors called a severe and sudden psychotic break, Aideen De Barra had been lost in a delusion that persuaded her that her husband of eighteen years, Elliot De Barra, had been turned into a vampire and wanted to kill his family.

As rich as they were, not even his parents' millions could keep the savage nature of his mam's actions from getting out, though the exact reasoning for the murder, that his mam staked her husband like in the movies, had been kept from all but the smallest of circles.

Even his younger sister Shauna was in the dark about it all.

But as Max had been the one to find his mam and call the guards, the image of seeing Aideen yanking the chair leg from his dad's chest, blood spattered all over her was something that Max could never erase from his mind.

Shauna didn't remember the events thankfully, and as her legal guardian, Max hoped she never would. At sixteen years old, Max hadn't been equipped to deal with the fallout, however his dad's best friend, and lawyer, Rodger White, had immediately filed a motion with the courts to grant Max emancipation, and guardianship of Shauna. The judge hadn't wanted to give a ten year old little girl to a sixteen year old boy, and yet, with the promise from Rodger that a full time personal assistant would be hired for Shauna while Max continued his schooling, and a mention of the many charitable donations from the De Barra's over the years, it was granted.

After the private funeral, Max had gone back to his boarding school, and Shauna to hers, but the boys that had been his friends now looked at him with equal parts curiosity, now that he was an overnight millionaire, and equal parts horror. He was sure they wondered if he too might be as fucking insane as his mother was.

Everyone had been waiting to see what exactly Max would do once he finished secondary school, and Rodger had told him that with the money he had now, he could travel the world for a bit and find his feet before he decided. But Max had left school and applied to the Irish Defence Forces before he'd even gotten his exam results. Max had spent two years in the defence forces. Then he had resigned in order to sign up to join the Garda so that he could spend more time in Ireland, be nearer to Shauna.

It was in becoming a Garda that Max found what he was truly good at. Like his father had been a brilliant architect, and his mother had excelled in her field, Max had, according to his training officer, had the most complex mind he had ever seen and that, Max would either be the best guard in Ireland or a prolific killer. Considering his mother was one of Ireland's most notable killers, streaming documentary and all, Max wasn't entirely sure that was a compliment.

Still, it meant that he quickly moved up the ranks and with his arrest record and case solving stats, Max had become one of the youngest Detective Sergeants in the entire country at twenty-four, was just over two years in the rank and Max was the person others called when they needed fresh eyes to help the catch the perpetrator.

He sold the mansion they had lived in, where their mam had killed their dad, and bought a smaller home that was situated on a hill, and had the highest of security.

Rodger had signed over all accounts to Max when Max returned from the army, and Max controlled Shauna's allowance, and would do until she was old enough. At twenty, Shauna was Max's opposite. She was rebellious, bucked against authority, and against Max at every turn, and had no idea what the real world was like.

If she didn't need Max to fund her rebellion, Max wasn't sure he'd even see Shauna at all.

Max shifted his gaze back toward the slain girl. Rían was carefully examining the victim, and Max could hear him whispering to the girl. When Max and Rían first started to work crime scenes together, Max had overheard some of the uniformed Garda talking shit about the way in which Rían talked to the dead. He had known Rían well enough to see that it had gotten to him, and Max didn't stand for it.

He had waited until everyone was back at the station, then in the dark outside in the car park, Max had cornered them both, and 'persuaded' them that the next time he heard them talking shit about the other man, he would make sure they were assigned to the traffic corps for the rest of their careers.

Max knew he could be an intensely scary bastard when he needed to be.

Rían had always joked with him that the reason why their school rugby team won so many matches was because even before the opposing team stepped onto the field, they were already scared of him. That facing down Maximillian De Barra was like standing in front of the All Blacks as they did the Hakka; you just knew you were fucked.

Turning his attention back to the murder scene, Max was just happy that it was a dry night, and the elements were not another thing to steal something from the dead girl. Once the influx of money had begun to flood into the city centre, the area around Grand Parade had been upgraded with heightened security and the laneways and interconnecting streets had been cleaned up and any and all elements that might have taken the expensive and shiny look of money off the street removed.

Tobin Street was a slender alleyway that linked Grand Parade to South Main Street if you didn't want to walk down Washington Street. It had once been filled with odd businesses and that, but now, since the rejuvenation, most of the businesses had been sold and while The Player's Lounge was the largest business at the mouth of Tobin Street, some smaller ones like a nail bar, a wine bar, and a spa that the guards were certain was offering more than just a cucumber facial to relax.

It was also one of the few places that the new security cameras didn't cover along the length of the alley. Rephrase that. In the beginning, cameras had been installed, but apart from the ones at the mouth at each end, the ones that would cover the club kept getting dismantled. Max would have to check and see if The Player's Lounge had any CCTV that showed the victim before and after she left the club.

The murderer would have to know that the cameras in the alleyway were non-existent, which meant they had known area, so had either scoped it out, or they called Cork their home.

Judging by the brutality of how the young woman was killed, the killer had done this before. The amount of blood alone suggested that they had plenty of time to rape and murder the girl. That spoke of either planning or recklessness, however from what looked like a lack of evidence so far at the crime scene, Max would bet the latter.

"Sir?"

The sound of the female Garda's voice dragged him from his thoughts, and he glanced over at her, saw her swallow hard.

"Sorry, sir, but I thought you might be interested in something I found out."

Max inclined his head, and the Garda continued. "Ms. McBride is the second employee from The Player's Lounge to end up deceased. Last week, a security staff member," She flipped the pages of her little notebook and then lifted her eyes back up to meet Max's, "Mark Shaw, was found dead in his apartment, fractured skull and he was ugh…"

The Garda blushed, like she couldn't say the words out loud, and Max sighed because if she couldn't say it now, then he knew the Garda would never be able to say it. She'd never work in sex crimes or homicide or anything that made her feel uncomfortable. It wasn't her fault; some people just couldn't compartmentalize.

Like you can compartmentalize what you saw in the kitchen that night your dad was murdered?

"Did the report say he was assaulted with a foreign object?"

The Garda paled, but she nodded, then hurried away when Max dismissed her. Turning his attention back to Rían, he noticed his friend was leaning in to get a closer look at the dead girl's neck. He reached for his camera, snapped a picture before he turned his attention to Max.

"What did ya find?"

"Two small puncture wounds on the neck. She also has a lot of healed marks in the area."

Max frowned. "Teeth?"

Rían shook his head, leaned back from the body. "I need a

better look back at the office, but I would think not teeth. Unless someone filed their gnashers to points like some vampire fetish."

"He was a fucking vampire, Max! I had to kill him."

Max sucked in a harsh breath as Rían looked at him, concern in his eyes and in his expression. Rían was one of the few people who knew all the sordid details of what happened that night and he opened his mouth to say something, but Max didn't need to hear Rían trying to offer him comfort.

He had a killer to find.

"I'm gonna go interview the owner of The Player's Lounge, see if they have CCTV, or can tell me anything about the two victims. Can you see who looked at Mark Shaw's crime scene and the body?"

Rían nodded, getting to his feet as Max headed back out of the street, his mind still on the puncture wounds on the girl's neck, and the awful thing his mother had done. Glancing at his watch, Max saw it was a quarter to one in the morning. The murdering hour still had time left in her.

THEO

W ell, this was a clusterfuck of epic proportions.

Theo watched as the guards and the pathologist work the scene outside her nightclub and frowned. For centuries she had prided herself on making sure herself and her Scion remained as inconspicuous as possible and now, two of her staff were dead.

If she found out that one of her vampires had decided to eat where they worked, she'd rip out their goddamn spines with her bare hands. It was her job as their Suzerain.

Taking in the scene below, Theo watched as the dark-haired male got to his feet, and headed out of the alleyway, stopping for a brief moment to look up toward the window in which Theo was looking out of, as if he had sensed her looking.

He couldn't see her, considering the privacy glass she had paid a fortune for allowed her to look out but kept people and most importantly the sun from getting inside.

Not that the sun bothered her much.

Movies and TV shows got a lot of shit wrong when it came to vampires.

Not all vampires were susceptible to the sun. Theo was a born vampire, a Velesan. The name was taken from the Slavic God of Alchemy. When vampires first roamed the earth, humans thought of them as Gods, and vampires, especially Velesan vampires, were so fucking full of themselves, they kept it.

Velesan vampires could walk in the sun, could eat and drink like a human, had a heartbeat and all that jazz. They aged until mid-late twenties and then they just stopped. A Velesan vampire was born only to a Velesan parent and either another Velesan or a human. They also inherited their powers from their sireline, though not necessarily inheriting the same powers as their parent.

Theo herself had inherited a power from her great, great, great grandfather.

Then there were the Zayan. Those were more like what the world perceived as vampires. They were human turned by Velesan or other Zayan, though the change was notoriously more successful if it was done by a Velesan. The Zayan essentially given back life. They gained immortality, strength, speed, and a sliver of power from the vampire who made them, but being brought back to life meant that the Zayan could not walk out into direct sunlight.

Though there were some anomalies, but that was for another day.

And vampires loved a power structure. In her Scion, Theo was the leader, not because she wanted the burden of being the head of a Scion, but because she was considered the strongest in the Scion, though her best friend Kaan wasn't far behind her. Kaan was her lieutenant, her second in command.

Kaan had been her friend for as long as Theo could remember, and there was many a time over her vast years that Theo might have sought death had it not been for the other Velesan. Their bond had been forged in blood and death, and not so easily dismissed.

Letting out a sigh, Theo reminded herself that she hated dwelling on the past. It never brought her any happiness and it certainly held not many fond memories.

Sometimes, legacy can be a curse.

Back when Theo had been born, a really long time ago, it was common practice for the first born Velesan of monarch and rulers to be taken from the parents and placed under the care of The Order of The Dragon to become a Paza, a bodyguard or a shield. Theo always used the word care loosely because what she had endured, what Kaan had endured and many others like her, was far from normal. Their birth was erased from records, and they became lost to history, even though they witnessed the most brutal of events.

From the moment Theo would walk, she was trained to fight, to use her powers both to attack and defend. The ironic thing about The Order of the Dragon was that all of the those chosen to be raised in the Order, including children of opposing monarchs were bunched together and trained to fight one another. It was a flaw in their teacher's thinking, because while you learned to make your opponent bleed and not flinch, it was also your opponent who tended to your wounds.

They were weapons, trained to protect the monarch if any attempts were made on the monarch's life. Their whole purpose was to step in and defend their monarch to the death. Theo had only seen her father from across the room at events. She knew who he was and who her mother had been, but her father had never acknowledged her.

Theo remembered one night when she had gotten as close to her father as possible. It was right outside the castle, high up on the hill as her father addressed his people. Theo had stood on the fringes, disguised as a villager, in awe of the man who ruled his country with a brutality that would make him infamous. She had lost that awe when her father had impaled men, women, and children on spikes for all to see.

Theo's father had been Vlad Țepeș, Voivode of Wallachia, better known to most as Vlad the Impaler or Vlad Dracul. And he had indeed been a vampire.

Her full proper name was Theodora Vladislava Tepes, prințesă of Wallachia.

Shaking her head from thinking of her infamous father, Theo focused on the possible catastrophe that could potentially mean her and the Scion moving. Ireland had been their home for the last couple of centuries and Theo hated packing up and setting up somewhere new.

Watching as Molly's body was zipped up into a body bag and lifted onto a stretcher, Theo frowned. She'd liked Molly. The young woman was working for Theo while attending college. Molly was aware that vampires existed. All of her employees were. They were told at the interview stage and any who freaked out or hesitated, Theo, or one of the other Velesan used compulsion to take the memory away.

Molly was also one of the staff who had taken Theo up on her offer to earn more money by donating blood to the vampires in her Scion. Some of the staff were open to donating to any other vampires who frequented The Player's Lounge and that meant a higher pay packet.

Because while Theo trusted the vampires in her inner circle of her Scion not to drain the staff to death, the same couldn't be said for other vampires who might overindulge. Most knew that Theo would be quick to decree their deaths if they swerved her rules.

She might not impale those who crossed her, but Theo showed no mercy to those who defied her edicts, because one slip, one deviation, could lead to an entire city being savaged.

A knock sounded on the door to her office, and Blair Ashcroft stuck her head in. The Velesan vampire was a good few centuries younger than her, had been Queen Victoria's distant cousin who had been given to The Order of The Dragon in England when Theo and Kaan had been already free of The Order.

She still had that regal grace to her that Theo had never learned, though the two-toned blonde and burgundy hair, and the accompanying tattoos had been Blair's rebellion once she too had gotten free of The Order. Considered the most successful of the Paza because Queen Victoria, a human who was deemed important enough to deserve the protection of the Order, reigned for sixty-three years.

"There's a guard downstairs looking to speak to you about Molly." Blair said in her aristocratic tone. "You better make an appearance before Kaan stirs up more trouble."

Theo rolled her eyes because making mischief was one of Kaan's favourite things to do. As if she read Theo's thoughts, Blair laughed, a lyrical sound and ducked back out leaving the door open for Theo to follow her out.

Theo's office was on the top floor of the building that they had gutted and renovated when creating The Player's Lounge. The building used to have five floors, but Theo had pushed for an attic conversion for her and Kaan's offices, plus a kitchen area and staff room for the Scion.

The top floor, right under her office, was the exclusive area. This was where vampires and humans paid for membership. The area was sectioned off into private rooms, and one communal area. The floor underneath the private rooms was a cigar lounge and had tables for gambling. The two floors below were the main floors of the nightclub and catered for a variety of different music tastes.

The main reception area that Theo was headed to had a waiting area, a lounge area, and a little bar. You also had to get passed the double doors to even get to the elevators that would take you to the floors your access wrist band got you. Below ground was basement level that catered to all vampires, and the humans who got off on being fed from. It was advertised as an exclusive nightclub area, and access was by invitation only.

Theo slipped into the elevator with Blair, leaned against the bars as she said to the other Velesan. "Who's down there keeping an eye on Kaan?"

Blair grinned. "Silas."

Considering that the hulking male had been made by Kaan, Theo knew the Zayan would stand by and watch as Kaan made a bad situation worse simply because it amused him.

Silas, Theo found, had a very strange sense of humour.

"Did we manage to clear out the basement before the guards showed up?" Theo asked, shifting forward on the balls of her feet.

Blair ran a hand through the burgundy side of her hair. "We did. When Simon realized a vampire had killed Molly, he radioed Silas who made sure anyone who was vampire was already gone before the first guard arrived. Silas would have taken Molly from the alleyway if the place hadn't been swarming with humans."

Whoever had killed Molly wanted her to be found and to stir things up. Theo would make sure that new cameras were installed in that alley. She wasn't sure she had the manpower to send members of her Scion out to watch out for the humans that worked for her, but with two dead employees, Theo knew she would have to do something.

When the elevator reached the reception floor, Blair strode out first and Theo followed after her. She could already hear Kaan and the guard arguing as she slipped out the door Blair held open for her, one of his uniformed police officers standing off to the side.

"As I said, I need to speak to the owner and not the middle management."

Theo almost laughed, knowing Kaan would hate being called middle management, and was unsurprised to hear the low growl that rumbled in Kaan's throat, and see the pissed off look on his face. The guard was standing with his back to Theo, and she was surprised at how causal he appeared.

Dressed in jeans, beat up sneakers, and a leather jacket, he wasn't like any guard that Theo had ever come across. He appeared young, his face when he had glanced up at her window had been handsome but not in an obvious way.

"The night is not getting any younger, Mr. Sydin. If your boss doesn't have the time to spare when two people have been murdered, then perhaps they have something to hide."

Theo halted where she was as Kaan arched an eyebrow at her.

"I can assure you that I have nothing to hide, Garda."

The guard turned slowly at the sound of her voice, then lowered his gaze to meet hers. His eyes were intense, dark, and piercing as they regarded her. Theo had stared a lot of people down but something told her that this man would not be intimidated by her in the slightest.

"I came to speak to Theo Caden. So, if you could stop messing me about and call him down here, we can all get on with our night."

Letting her lips curve into a smirk, Theo tilted her head and extended her hand. "I'm sorry, did I forget to introduce myself? I'm Theodora Caden, Theo for short."

The slight arch of one of his brows was the only change to his expression as the guard remarked as he shook her hand, "How does someone as young as you afford an establishment like this?"

Well, wasn't he just a condescending prick...

Theo removed her hand and gave the guard her haughtiest

glare as she said. "Despite having an absentee father, he left me a fuckton of money when he did the world a favour and died. Sometimes having a legacy can be a good thing."

Kaan made a choking sound behind the guard, and even Silas had taken to covering his mouth to stop from laughing.

"Ms. Caden,"

"Theo. Just Theo."

The guard still looked at her like he was trying to delve deep into her soul. "Ms. Caden, two of your employees are dead. One right outside her place of work. Do you know of anyone who might have a vendetta against you or your establishment?"

"If there was, I of course would tell you, Garda…"

Theo wanted to know who this guard was, and just how good of a job he might do investigating these crimes. He had intelligent eyes, curious and suspicious at the same time. But knowing his name would be a start to having members of the Scion run a check on him.

"Detective Sergeant De Barra."

This time, Theo arched her brow. "Awfully young to be a Detective Sergeant, aren't you?"

The Detective Sergeant smirked. "As you said, sometimes legacy is a good thing."

While most might have assumed that his comment was a flyaway remark that nepotism had gotten him where he was, Theo could tell that his comment hadn't been that. Fuck, why did he have to make himself interesting?

"I'm sure my head of security has already offered to hand over any CCTV that we have that might lead to Molly's killer. We will get that to you as soon as possible." Theo told him, as the guard slipped his hands into his pockets.

"Hopefully all the CCTV will be intact when we do receive it, Ms. Caden."

"Oh, I hope so too, Detective Sergeant. Alas, technology is not infallible."

Theo tilted her head and starred into the Detective's eyes. She pushed power into her gaze to compel him, to avert his attention elsewhere.

"You will find no evidence here that we participated in the murder. You really need to look elsewhere."

Theo waited for the telltale glassy expression as the compulsion settled it.

The Detective blinked, gave her an amused expression. "I'll be the judge of that Ms. Caden. Don't leave town."

What the actual fuck?

Turning away from Theo, Detective Sergeant De Barra headed out the main door, Kaan blowing him a kiss before he strode over to the bar and grabbed a beer. He opened his mouth to speak but Theo shook her head to warn him to stay quiet for the moment.

Theo was certain it wouldn't be the last that they saw of Detective Sergeant De Barra.

"I see you've met Detective Dracula."

Theo whirled round to stare at the uniformed Garda. Kaan spat out his beer and Silas was busting a gut laughing. They all stared at the guard, who shifted uncomfortably under their scrutiny.

"I beg your fucking pardon?" Theo said, her heart racing at what might come next from the man's mouth.

"Um, ya," The guard said with a snort. "Everyone at the station calls him, Detective Dracula. It's cause he only works the night shift, rarely seen in daylight. Max prefers to work alone. Likes working murders like some people like doing crossword puzzles. Everyone thinks he's secretly a vampire."

"Is that so?" Kaan drawled, the amusement in his tone meant that he would tease Theo about it a lot.

"Ya, sure is." The human confirmed. "When he got promoted to Detective Sergeant, his teammates cooked pasta with lots of garlic in it, just to see if he could eat it."

Garlic was another myth that the humans got wrong.

Theo herself was very fond of garlic.

"And did he eat it?" Kaan asked.

"Oh ya, even went back for seconds in all."

Silas distracted the guard to allow Theo, Kaan, and Blair to escape. Once inside the elevator, Theo looked at Kaan and motioned with her hand. "Okay come on, you look like you are about to burst if you don't say shit so get it off your chest."

Kaan gave her his most charming smile, and Theo could see why men and women wanted to worship him. His sun-kissed skin was a mark of his Turkish heritage. His dark hair that always looked like he'd just rolled out of bed, and he had mischievous eyes to go with his devilish good looks. He was tall and slender, but his training had afforded him with washboard abs that he liked to show off in expensive clothing.

They should have been mortal enemies, Theo and Kaan, because his father had been the Turkish Ottoman her father had been at war with.

Instead, it had brought them closer together.

"Theo, darling, I would never dare infer that perhaps the Gods had finally delivered to you a man who might end your dry spell."

"He's investigating a murder, and he's an asshole, Kaan."

Kaan's smile deepened, dimpling his cheeks. "Detective Dracula. Now, that's the most amusement I've had in weeks."

"Fuck off, Kaan. You're an asshole too."

The elevator stopped to let Kaan out as he strode over and kissed the top of Theo's head. "But you still love me, Theo. Even if I am an asshole."

Theo flipped him off, which drew a chuckle from Kaan. Blair stepped off the elevator as well, pausing when Theo asked Blair to have the Scion meet at the house they shared just after sunset. Blair gave her a salute and then the doors closed, leaving Theo alone.

It's happening again...

Theo tried not to think the worst but when you lived as long as she had, you grew to expect it. More time in this world meant you had more time to amass enemies, and hell, she had a few. Theo might not have wanted to be the Suzerain of the Scion, but she was and she needed to protect them against any threats to their safety.

 **MAX**

Max arrived home a little after nine two days after the murder at The Player's Lounge and tossed his keys on the side table as he shut the front door behind him. The De Barra estate on the outskirts of Cork City was an extensive property that was surrounded by walls that kept the public out. Max and his sister had moved in not long after he had joined the Garda, believing a new house and home would ensure Shauna had the semblance of normality that she needed.

His sister had instead taken her anger out on Max for selling the family home and trying to brush aside the evilness of their mam's act. Shauna had decided that despite their mam's illness, that Aideen was dead to her and she hated that Max still was available to visit their mam when he had time.

And since neither Aideen nor Elliot De Barra were around for Shauna to take her anger out on, Max bore the brunt of the tumultuous swirl of emotions that was hardly ever contained in his sister.

"Shauna," he called up the stairs as he did every morning when he got home. "You home?"

The silence that greeted him was nothing new. It didn't matter if his sister was at home, the arctic blast that usually followed his sister where he was concerned was the same. Shauna made it her business to be gone from the house when she knew Max was likely to be home. On the rare occasions when Max made it home prior to Shauna leaving for college, his sister would just cast him a glare, ask when her next inheritance payment was due as if she wanted to remind him that the only reason she stuck around was because Max controlled the purse strings.

Max shook his head as he strode through the reception area of the house and into the kitchen. He grabbed a bottle of water from the fridge before walking back out of the kitchen and gave a low whistle. There was the sound of paws on the stairs and his German Shepherd, JD, rounded the corner. JD was highly trained and would know the sound of his car and the cadence of his steps so knew to only come once Max called for him.

But he pitied the fucking idiot who tried to break into this house when Max wasn't here.

"Hey buddy." Max said to the dog as he walked back to the kitchen, opened the sliding door for JD to let him out.

When Max had been in the defence forces, on one of their peace keeping missions, JD's previous handler had been killed in action, and JD was due to be retired, but JD had alerted Max when there was an attempted ambush during the body retrievals, and Max had then paid a massive amount to bring JD home with him.

Once JD was back inside, Max yawned and called JD to him as he went up the stairs, heading toward his side of the house. It was one of the things that had appealed to Max about the house when he had bought it, trying to show Shauna that she could have some privacy by having her own side, completely separate from Max's.

Shauna had proceeded to test Max's theory by blaring her music loud enough to wake the dead.

Pushing open the door to his bedroom, Max took off his jacket and threw it on the back of the chair as he went to close the blinds. JD curled up on his dog bed, huffing out a snort as he did. Once the room was suitable darkened, Max stared at the bed and wondered why he even bothered trying to sleep. He always went through the motions. He darkened the room, stripped off his clothes, got under the covers and lay down staring at the ceiling.

Most days, sleep evaded him. Others, he was haunted by nightmares of the night his father had died. The shrink he paid and visited at least once a month if not on a case told Max that he had a sleep disorder and prescribed him sleeping tablets. Max never took them. He hated the way they made him feel and how groggy his brain felt for days afterward.

His mind was too full of murder today to get any useful sleep but he knew that when he went to see Rían later on after the autopsy, and his friend noted the dark circles under his eyes, that Rían would try to get him to take a break from work.

The last time Rían had suggested that Max take a holiday, Max had just snorted and asked Rían what exactly he expected Max to do on holiday. Rían had suggested he do some sunbathing, played some golf, or something. His friend had then retorted that it might be a good idea if Max got laid, since it had been a while.

Max had only rolled his eyes, flipped him off, and told Rían to be more concerned about his own sex life. He didn't have time in his life to be in a relationship or to even bother with casual hook ups. In Max's attempts to try and give Shauna a normal life, Max had dated a woman on his return from the defence forces. He'd stupidly thought having a woman in Shauna's life would make it easier for his sister and yet, it had only made it harder for Max.

Most people didn't get him. Vanessa certainly hadn't and Max was the first to admit that he hadn't gotten Vanessa either. He'd dated her because Max had felt she fit a profile. She came from a wealthy family. Her parents and his had been friends. She was good with Shauna, had her own job to keep her occupied, and fit the type of woman his mother would have liked for him.

Max had been utterly bored with it all and had started to spend more and more time at work, meaning Vanessa got pissed off with him a lot. Max wanted to stay out of the limelight, while Vanessa urged him to take advantage of his infamous parents. Vanessa had wanted more from Max than he could give her. She'd wanted the ring, and the house, and babies. She had wanted Max to stand beside her on red carpets and go to Galas, but he had made himself unavailable. Then when she mentioned marriage, Max had told Vanessa he wasn't the marrying kind, so Vanessa had then made a pass at Rían in front of Max to make him jealous.

But Max hadn't given a fuck so Vanessa had packed up her shit and left.

Max hadn't felt anything but relief.

"If I didn't know any better, Max, I'd think you were dead inside."

That's what Rían had said to him when he'd come over after Vanessa had left and Max had just shrugged when Rían had asked him if he was good. His therapist told him plenty of times that he was excellent at keeping his emotions at bay.

Hell, Max couldn't remember the last time he had done something just for fun.

Although today trading barbs with his number one suspect Theodora Caden had sparked something inside him. He normally noticed things about people. Tells. Minute little details that gave away a person but today he had noticed Theo Caden's almost subdued beauty under all that orange hair.

Deciding that the last thing Max needed to do was focus on any attraction to the mysterious woman, he lay staring at the ceiling, exhaustion settling into his bones, a sense of wrongness in the pit of his stomach as he closed his eyes.

Max rolled his eyes as he got out of the back seat of Rían's Mercedes and his best friend shouted at him that he would never get laid if he didn't smile more. He flipped Rían off, that gnawing feeling in the pit of his stomach that had come upon him suddenly and urged him to go home.

As Rían peeled out of the driveway, Max glanced down at his watch to see it was dead on midnight. The uneasy sensation in his stomach had amplified as they drew nearer to his home, and now, it felt like he was about to throw up on his mam's flower bed.

He'd only had like two beers, so Max knew he wasn't drunk or anything.

Maybe he was coming down with a stomach bug or something.

Slipping his hand into his pocket, Max took out his keys and unlocked the door. The house was shrouded in darkness, the only light was coming from the crack under the kitchen door. The clenching in his stomach became stronger as Max took a step forward into the hall.

Tilting his head, Max could hear his little sister crying in her room. It was unusual for Shauna to be awake this late, and that should have been Max's first clue that something was terribly wrong. He contemplated going to check on Shauna, but every instinct in his body was screaming at him to go to the kitchen.

With every step Max took toward the kitchen, the more his stomach threatened to revolt.

His hands trembled as he pushed open the door. There was a crash from inside and his heart was racing so loud that he almost missed the sound of a snarl as his head snapped round and he sucked in a breath.

His dad was on his back on the floor, and his mam was straddling his waist. There was a broken chair to the right of them and as Max fought the urge not to vomit, he noted that one of the legs of the chair was lodged in his dad's chest, his mam's grip on the wooden piece holding it there.

His mam yanked the wood right out as if it was nothing as she tilted her head and looked at the man she had been married to for almost two decades. Max was frozen to the spot, the uneasy sensation dissipating in his stomach.

"Mam?" He heard himself saying as his mam whipped her head round.

There was a wildness in her eyes that Max had never seen before. Her hair was dishevelled, and her clothing torn. She had blood dripping down her arms and a cut to her face. The only way that Max could describe her face was feral.

Her features softened when she looked at him. She leaned back, then jumped to her feet with a grace that surprised Max into taking a step back.

"Max, my love." She started, sounding like his mam but he was struggling to believe what he had just seen. His mother had murdered his father. His father was lying dead on the floor.

"You felt it, didn't you?" She continued, that creepy smile curving her lips. "You felt it in your bones and came home. My son. My legacy. It's in our blood."

Max couldn't speak, the words were lodged in his throat. His mam had lost it. Gone completely postal and now his dad, who

Max loved, was dead on the floor. What was he even doing here? His dad was supposed to be overseas working on a new build.

His mam glanced down at her husband, then back at Max. "He chose evil, Max. He chose to become a vampire and I had to kill him. You understand, right? It is in our blood to hunt and kill vampires."

Well, now Max really knew his mam had gone insane...she thought her husband was a vampire.

"Mam, there is no such thing as vampires."

His mam laughed, the sound so eery the hairs on the back of his neck stood to attention. "One day... one day you will understand, and you will know. That monster was no longer the man I loved. He would have killed me. Killed you and your sister because he chose to become a vampire when he knew I would kill him."

Sirens blared from the distance and Max glanced at the door and back, his mam moving with speed as she dropped the chair leg to the ground and placed her bloody hands on either side of Max's face. "I can hear it in you, singing to me, Max. One day you will understand."

Max opened his mouth to speak but the front door burst open. Guards stormed in shouting as his mam shoved away from him and dropped to her knees. He was powerless to do anything as his mam was cuffed and dragged away, all the while screaming at him about vampires.

Max bolted upright in bed, panic clutching his chest as he tried to reign in the affect the memories of that night always brought. Pressing his fists to his eyes, he tried to push the images from his mind until his heart stopped racing.

His mam told him all the time that he was just like her, his dad too. Max himself had never seen it himself, and he didn't care. What got to Max the most was if he had listened to his gut sooner, if he'd been more insistent that Rían take him home, or hell, called a cab to bring him home, could those extra few minutes have saved his dad's life?

And if he had paid closer attention to his mam's behaviour, could he have prevented his mam from having such a violent breakdown?

Shaking away the memories of that terrible night, though they never did quite leave Max alone, he got out of bed, noting that he had only slept a few hours. With a heavy sigh, Max pulled on some shorts and a tee, slipped on his running shoes, and whistled for JD to follow him.

Rían teased Max for his love of running, that it was boring, but with his headphones on and the feel of the concrete beneath his feet, running helped Max focus and clear his mind. Before everything happened, Max had been on the track team in school, and aspired of maybe one day heading to the Olympics. But he'd given it all up when track meets became a media circus with reporters trying to get the scoop on his mam, and his dad's murder.

Putting on his headphones and connecting them to his phone, Max put on his running playlist and headed out the door after grabbing JD's leash, would clip it on when he got to a busier place. It wasn't exactly legal, but Max didn't care. He jogged at a steady pace as he went down the driveway, pressed the button on his phone to open the gate and then lost himself in the music and the run.

JD ran beside him as they went down the hill and along the streets. It was early afternoon in Cork City, so it was busy enough. He jogged through the streets, clipping on JD's leash in the populated areas. Max slowed his pace as he crossed the road and looked over to The Player's Lounge. It was too early for the bar to be open fully, and the main clientele that frequented the establishment did so at night.

The alleyway was still cordoned off with a Garda standing at the mouth allowing business owners to duck under the cordon. A wave of unease swayed in his stomach, urging him to go inside, to follow the invisible thread that seemed to want to yank him toward The Player's Lounge.

Resisting the urge, Max headed off on his run again, and the uneasy sensation started to dissipate. As afternoon started to draw in, Max headed home, the muscles in his calves burning as he climbed the hill and ducked inside the gates.

Awareness prickled his senses.

Darting his gaze around the courtyard, Max couldn't shake the feeling that he was being watched. He glanced toward the woodland area, narrowing his eyes as he stared at the trees. The branches swayed, the wind picking up, but although Max could *feel* eyes on him, he couldn't make sense of why he would think that someone was lurking in the trees, watching him.

You've felt these feelings before....

The front gates opened, and Shauna drove her Mini Cooper in, barely sparing him a glance as she parked next to his Land Rover. His sister got out of her car, and glared at Max. Her black and blue hair was loose around her shoulders, a beanie cap on her head. Shauna was wearing jeans and a tee that said, *Parental Advisory- Explicit Content.* Her rebellion against Max meant she had gotten an array of tattoos and piercings that Max stopped commenting on when he realized she was doing it because it annoyed him.

He wasn't opposed to body art even had some ink himself... he just hated how impulsive Shauna was.

Being impulsive could get you killed.

Having grabbed her backpack from the boot, Shauna made to walk inside, glaring at him still, though she did stop to give JD a scratch behind the ears.

"Hey, I was just gonna cook something to eat before work... you wanna have dinner with me? You can tell me how college is going." Max asked Shauna as he did most days when their paths eventually crossed.

Shauna pursed her lips, like she was thinking about it, then flipped her hair off her shoulder, giving him this up yours expression. "Nah, not in the humour for a Max lecture today. I'll eat when you've fucked off to work."

She punctuated her point by sauntering to the front door and slamming it closed in her wake. A few minutes later, Max heard the pulse of music coming from inside the house.

JD nudged his leg and Max reached down to scratch behind his ears. "Come on, buddy, let's go have dinner."

Keeping an eye on the trees, Max felt the unease in his

stomach start to fade, and when he paused in the archway of the door to look dead at the point in the trees where he had felt eyes on him, it was gone.

# THEO

Parking her car in the car port, Theo got out and grabbed her bag before heading inside. It was almost sunset, and Theo hadn't been home since the murder at The Player's Lounge. She was exhausted and hungry for food, having sated her blood hunger with one of the donors at the club. The made vampires would be getting up soon and Theo always enjoyed the little semblance of quiet just before chaos normally ensued.

Theo had a pounding headache as she shut the front door of the place she and the Scion had called home since they settled in Ireland almost five hundred years ago. Once a wealthy landowner's estate, Theo and Kaan had purchased it so that all of the Scion could live under one roof. A lot of the Scion came and went, but her inner circle, the ones she trusted the most, they lived here with her.

Over the years, Theo had been approached by various luxury hotel chains looking to purchase the property, but they always left disappointed. There were several acres of land surrounding the house that was enclosed by woods and a tall wall blocked the view from any passersby. The long driveway up to the main building wove around in a circle.

Ivy crept up the walls of the house, Silas tending to it as he did a lot of the plants and flowers in the surrounding areas. He might look like a brute of a man, but he was very gentle when it came to his flowers...and a certain blonde-haired vampire.

Tossing her keys on the sideboard after she walked into the foyer, Theo dropped her bag, crossed the foyer, and turned right to head down the hall to where the kitchen was. Someone had made coffee and left it in the pot, so she poured herself a cup and perched up on the breakfast counter and took a moment to herself.

Everything had been utter madness since Molly's murder. Gardaí waltz in and out of The Player's Lounge like they owned the place and even now that they had cleared off to continue their investigation, they had left one lone uniformed Garda standing at the mouth of the alleyway.

That had killed her business for the next night...

Pardon the pun.

Theo had gone with Kaan to see Molly's parents. It always amazed Theo how loving parents were supposed to be. She never had that. Her father was who he was and her mother, well, if Theo was right, her mother had thrown herself off a cliff rather than stay married to her father.

Had she even known Theo was alive?

Of course, they had offered to pay for Molly's funeral and anything else the family needed. Molly's mam had hugged her, told her how much Molly liked working at The Player's Lounge, liked her bosses. She had babbled on for ages until Kaan used a little gentle persuasion to wrap things up.

That made Theo think of the Detective Sergeant who had blinked away her compulsion like she had no power at all. He had been human. His scent gave nothing away that he might be anything but human. While it wasn't unknown for some strong-willed humans to be able to shake off the compulsion from the less powerful Zayan, there was no way an ordinary human could have done that with a Velesan.

Shortly after Detective Sergeant De Barra had walked away from them, and after Kaan had stopped taking the piss out of her for the Detective Dracula joke, Theo knew she had to find out all she could about the man who she couldn't fucking compel..

Kaan had been the one to suggest that they send Kannon to spy on the Detective during the daylight hours. As Kannon had been made by Kaan, and powers could manifest in ways similar to a sire like Kannon's had. Kannon was one of the few Zayan who could tolerate being out in the sun for a period of time.

Japanese by birth, Kannon had been working as a hustler to

survive, picking pockets of tourists, and counting cards. He was also working for the Yakuza and had the misfortune of trying to fleece the wrong person. Kaan had been at the poker table that night and followed Kannon, watched as he was shot, then made him into a vampire.

And those two had been dancing around their feelings for one another for as long as Kannon had been a vampire...half a century.

Theo had also called their resident tech guru, Maisie, to do a full background check on Detective Sergeant De Barra. A Zayan made by Theo's former mentor Valerian, Maisie had the ability to touch any tech, whether it was a mobile phone or a missile, and know how to use it, but only if someone with that knowledge had touched it previously.

Her maker, Valerian, had been the weapons master of their chapter of The Order of the Dragon, and he had been able to wield any weapon known to man, once it had been touched by someone who knew how to use it. If it was a brand-new weapon, Valerian wouldn't know how to use it until someone competent touched it first.

Powers were weird, and they always came with a catch...it was like the universe was trying to balance shit out.

Footsteps sounded on the back stairs and Theo scented Kaan coming into the kitchen. He was dressed in silk pyjamas; the buttons open on the front displaying his golden-brown skin and a cheeky smile on his face.

Reaching out, he swiped the coffee from her grasp and lifted it to his lips.

"Hey! Get your own coffee. Some of us haven't even gone to bed yet."

Kaan chuckled, then went to pour Theo a fresh cup before sliding it across to her. She caught it with ease, then accepted the chocolate bar that he'd nabbed from her stash in the fridge. Not exactly a nutritious dinner but hey, it would keep her going until someone made some actual food.

"Kannon messaged me a while ago. Said there is definitely something with your Detective Dracula."

Theo rolled her eyes. "Fuck off. Was that all he said?"

Kaan nodded, took a sip from his stolen coffee before replying. "Yup. Said he'd explain once he got home. Maisie should be down soon to go through what she found about your Detective too."

"He's not my Detective, Kaan." Theo snarled, getting a little annoyed now to go with her tired.

Kaan opened his mouth to retort when Maisie staggered into the kitchen looking like she had gotten as much sleep as Theo had. She clutched a tablet to her chest as she yawned. "Please tell me there is coffee."

The youngest of all the Zayan, Maisie Clarke had been made a vampire just five years ago. Twenty-three when she was reborn, she had pale blue eyes and ash blonde hair. Slim but with curves, and legs that were long and lean, Maisie looked like she should be in college doing some arty type of course. She had an array of tattoos and piercings, and a cheeky smile and sense of humour that reminded Theo of how young she was.

Once Maisie had been suitably caffeinated, she climbed onto a stool and began swiping through her tablet. "Detective Sergeant Maximillian, Elliot, Senan De Barra is twenty-six years old and a taurus. Left school and joined the Defence Forces, then joined the Gardai so that he could be around to look after his younger sister. Father deceased. Mother's in a residential home."

There was a twinkle in Maisie's eyes and Kaan noticed it to because he nudged her shoulder so that she would go on. Maisie sighed very dramatically before continuing.

"There was an incident in the family home when Max was sixteen and while most people would not have been able to get passed the firewall to unseal the sealed file, I of course being a genius, did just that."

Maisie grinned, taking a sip of her coffee before swiping at her tablet. "Max came home to find that his mother had gone mad and murdered his father by driving a leg of a chair through his heart. The records state that Aideen De Barra, was raving about her husband Elliot being a vampire."

Theo and Kaan exchanged a look. They kept track of any

vampires made by them or any of the Scion. Elliot De Barra was not on their records.

"Elliot, used to have a different surname and looks like he took the wife's name when they got hitched. The records were sealed after a sizable donation from the De Barra foundation."

Had Max's mam actually killed a vampire or was she ill?

"Oh wait, that isn't even the juiciest part! Do you guys remember that vampire two years ago who was kidnapping all those kids and his power meant we couldn't find him?"

How could Theo forget. Erasmus Finn had been hiding in her territory unbeknownst to the Scion. He had kidnapped and killed a number of children, until he was caught and killed by the guards. Theo and Kaan had made sure he was dead, dead, and not just pretending.

Maisie propped up her tablet, enlarging a video that Theo knew just from looking at it that Maisie had acquired it through not so legal means. In the image on the tablet, Theo saw a younger version of Max sitting behind a desk, his fists clenched on the desk. He was dressed in full Garda uniform. Max was clean shaven, which made Theo think that she preferred the stubbled look he was wearing now.

Theo frowned, knowing that there was nothing good to come of Theo having a preference to Max's appearance.

Focusing on the video on the tablet, Theo inclined her head indicating Maisie should press play.

"Garda De Barra, can you tell us how you came across Mr. Finn and the kidnapped girl?" Asked a voice off camera.

Max stared at the camera for a second before he swallowed hard and began to speak. "Dumb luck, I guess."

Kaan snorted. "Oh, Detective Dracula is lying his ass off."

Theo glared at him to shut up as another voice said in a coaxing manner. "Come on now, Max. Tell the nice people at internal affairs what you told me. Come on now, lad. They think you were in on it."

Theo watched as Max's knuckles clenched and went white. "I'm not fucking crazy."

"We know that lad. But the truth is better than them thinking you killed a bunch of kids now, isn't it?"

Max leaned back in his chair, folding his arms across his chest, but he didn't say anything.

"I'll ask you again, Garda De Barra, how did you know where Finn was?"

"I just did." Came a grunted response and someone off camera sighed.

"Max, they want to string ya up and put ya in prison lad. Come on now. Stop being a stubborn donkey."

There was a silence of a couple of heartbeats and then Max spoke so quietly, if not for their preternatural hearing, Theo might have missed it.

"I felt it in my gut."

"Excuse me?" The internal affairs officer asked.

Lead weighed down in Theo's stomach.

"I was driving past on my way home from dinner and there was this pain in my stomach. It went away after I drove past the house. So, I went back and the pain it was screaming at me. I walked up and rang the doorbell and when Finn opened the door, I knew he was the monster we were looking for."

"And what happened next?"

Max shifted slightly in his seat like he was uncomfortable. "I told Finn that I was driving by and got a flat tyre, and my phone was dead. Asked him if he had a mobile, I could use to call my breakdown company. He let me in. I spotted the pink bunny that was taken with the girl. It was front and centre of all the other toys he was keeping as trophies."

"What happened then, Garda De Barra?"

"Finn realized that I had him sussed. He lunged for me. Fucker was fast and strong. But I tripped him, and he stumbled. We grappled and I shoved him hard into the coat hanger on the wall. It went right through his chest."

Was it dumb luck or inherited skill? That's what Theo wanted to know.

"Can you explain then why you drove a kitchen knife into his heart? Seems like overkill."

"The hook went centre mass. I was making sure the fucker didn't get back up."

Theo heard a snort as she leaned forward as if she needed to get a closer look at Max.

"And the knife you used was your own, correct? An illegal hunting knife."

Max tilted his head, his face expressionless as he arched a brow. "Does that really matter? We've been chasing Finn for months. I found him. He's dead and the latest child he took is reunited with their parents. Good news story for the force, right? Who the hell cares if the knife I used was my personal one. Take the win."

"Max." The other Garda sighed in a chastising tone. "Go and get yourself cleaned up, lad."

Max rose off the chair, gave a little salute and then he was gone from the room, but the camera was still recording.

"Christ, Mike, that kid is a massive pain in the ass. You believe his story?"

"Hundred per cent, Alan. You haven't seen him. Aced all his physical tests. Nailed all the knowledge tests. It was like the kid was born to solve crimes. He sees things no one else does. That prostitute ring last year? He put all the pieces we were missing together. He stared at the board for like an hour, without moving and that was it. Two hours later we had the pimps in custody."

Maisie leaned forward and pressed stop. "Are you thinking what I'm thinking?"

It was entirely plausible that Max De Barra was a Cathainite.

The Cathainites were descendants of one of the very first vampire hunters. Other countries had their own fables, but they all were created from the same lore. Theo had learned about all of the different vampire lore's growing up under the watch of the Order of the Dragon, and last she had heard, there was only a few small smatterings of people who still called themselves Cathainites.

Ireland had a legend that was much more intricately linked to truth of vampires. In this story, the vampire was called the Abhartach. The creature was killed and buried. But the Abhartach was not truly dead, merely wounded. It escaped from its grave to hunt for fresh blood.

In this story, a chieftain who goes by the name of Cathain consults a Saint. The Saint told Cathain that the only way to kill the Vampire was to find a sword made from yew wood. The Saint advised Cathain that, once the Abhartach was killed, he would need to bury him upside down and that he would need to find a great stone to lock it in for good.

The story ended with Cathain having easily killed the Abhartach and as per the Saint, after burying it nearby, he hoisted a heavy stone over the grave to keep the Abhartach in place.

That was only part of the story, however. Cathain had spoken with a Saint and a druid. The druid had told Cathain that the only way to defeat the Abhartach was to become as strong as it, as fast as it, as thirsty for death as it was...and through magic, Cathain was given the power to defeat the creature of the night.

For centuries, the descendants of Cathain were drawn to vampires. Compelled to kill them.

And if Max was a descendant of Cathain, his instincts would be telling him that there was something about her Scion. He'd be like a dog with a bone once he realized what they were...that's if he even knew what he was.

A hunter never stopped the pursuit of its prey once the hunt had begun.

And the same could be said for vampires.

But it didn't matter whether they were Cathainites or some other branch of hunter, they were all the fucking same.

Self-righteous pricks.

Theo had killed her fair share of hunters. If there was a most wanted list of vampires that the hunters wanted to kill, she would be at the very top. The fact that her father was who he was, made her a sort of celebrity, and a valuable commodity to hunters and vampires alike.

"Does he know what he is?" Theo asked softly, lifting her gaze to Maisie.

The young vampire shook her head. "Doesn't look like it. Most Cathainites come into their power at eighteen, but parents usually start training them from like sixteen, right? His dad was dead by then and his mam in a mental health facility. There is every possibly that he has no clue about himself or us."

Kaan got up and poured himself another coffee. "Then we kill him. One less hunter in the world has got to be a good thing."

That was the most logical thing to do considering all the options, but Theo felt uneasy about killing Max just because of his heritage. Wasn't that justifying all the people who wanted her dead because of who her father was?

"Oh no, I recognise that look."

Theo flipped Kaan off, rolling her eyes. "What look?"

"The bleeding-heart look. You might be as bloodthirsty as they come, darling, but that heart of yours will give you wrinkles from all the stress."

Theo got up and rubbed her temples, shaking her head. "Well murder plotting can wait until I've at least had a few hours' sleep. Don't wake me unless something or someone is on fire."

Kaan and Maisie laughed as she left them in the kitchen and headed up to her bedroom. Her room, as well as Kaan's were situated on the top floor with enough distance away for privacy. When she reached the top step, she saw that there was already a creature waiting at her door for her.

"Hey fat cat."

Said fat cat, whose name was Louis, after a certain movie vampire, gave her this annoyed look, hissed, and flashed his own fangs at her as she opened her bedroom door, before he sauntered inside like he owned the place.

Fucking asshole cat.

MAX

Having showered and dressed for work, Max still couldn't shake the feeling that he was being watched. It was faint now, like an itch he needed to scratch. Or a fly that kept on buzzing around him. Not wanting to alarm Shauna, he sent an email to the security team who monitored the house and told them to keep an eye on his sister if she ventured out that night.

If Shauna knew that he always kept eyes on her, she'd rage at him. Max knew that he was being over cautious and overprotective, but every couple of years the story of his father's murder became a hot topic, and that meant Shauna was in the spotlight once more.

Max hoped for the best but prepared for the worst.

His drive to work was short, delayed only when Max stopped off to put diesel in his car and grab all the morning newspapers. Rían took the piss out of him, telling him that most newspapers were all online now. But Max preferred to sit down with a coffee and read an actual physical copy to see if any details he might have missed were in those pages.

Max remembered that his dad had been the same way. Elliot had the same routine every day. He got up at six in the morning, put on a pot of coffee, then walked down the path to the post box to collect the newspapers that had been delivered. He came back in and poured himself a black coffee, made some toast and then sat at the kitchen table as he perused through the newspapers.

At seven-thirty on the dot, his dad closed his newspaper, put his things on the side and went into his home office to start work.

His mam had spent a lot of time away. As an antiques broker,

Aideen was frequently travelling, but his dad was the one who was stay at home even if he had a steady stream of work. He usually went out for meetings a couple of times a week but was always back in time to make sure he and Shauna had a parent to sit down to dinner with whenever they were home at the weekends or during midterms and holidays.

Maybe that's why Max was killing himself trying to get Shauna to have a meal with him?

Pulling into the station, Max parked his Land Rover in the first available space. Getting out, Max grabbed his newspapers and the coffee he'd gotten from the petrol station. He inclined his head to a few Garda who greeted him, then went straight through the main hub to his office.

Max closed the door behind him, then sat down behind his desk and went through his newspapers. The murders were front page news. Pictures of the victim were plastered among the headlines. There was even a picture of him and Rían at the crime scene on one paper, which also included that fucking picture of him walking out of Erasmus Finn's house with the girl in his arms.

Rían had somehow gotten hold of the original photo and had it framed for Max.

Max rolled his eyes as he read the headline on the newspaper. *Hero who thwarted child killer and saved young child investigating murder of young student outside exclusive nightclub.*

Well, as annoying as the headline was, at least it didn't say something like son of Cork's most notorious killer investigating murder of young woman or some shit. Though Max supposed that would come soon if the killer wasn't found quickly or there were more bodies.

When he had finished with the papers, Max took off his leather jacket and set it on the back of his chair. Grabbing his coffee, he strode out of his office and into the incident room. The room was messy, no doubt from the day shift but Max was glad that no one had touched his board.

While Max would have been quite happy to work on the case himself, his boss Mike O'Connor, was adamant that crimes didn't get solved by one person, even if Max had pointed out that he closed more cases by himself than entire teams.

He wasn't that much of a people person.

Turning his attention to the board on the wall, he scanned the information that he'd written on it the previous night. There was a profile of each of the two victims, Molly, and Mark, along with facts they knew about the murders. Max had noted down things like how the murder had taken place on the first dry night of the month, like the killer had planned for the body to be found.

There was blood under the girl's finger nails, and Max was too cynical to think that they'd get a hit. If the killer was as meticulous as Max believed, then any evidence left on the body was going to be either something the murderer wanted them to find, or something that would be no help to them whatsoever and would just take up time and resources.

This was not the first time that the killer Max was hunting had done this. Of that he was certain, like he could feel it in his bones.

Max slid his gaze toward another set of photos on the board. Theodora Caden had vivid green eyes that illuminated her entire face. Her hair was not naturally orange. It made Max curious to know what colour it had been originally. In the picture, her lips were curved into a smile.

Her business partner, the man who was of eastern European descent, Kaan Sydin had tried to unnerve him with his flirting tone, but Max didn't care too much about all that. He had known that Mr. Sydin had been only trying to delay him talking to Theo.

It had made him more suspicious of the nightclub and all who worked inside it. As certain as Max was that the killer had been killing for a while, he was certain that the woman who owned The Player's Lounge knew more than she was letting on.

Max knew that the club catered for exclusive clients as well as ordinary people, and he had noted the sign in the entrance to the club.

Welcome to The Player's Lounge - Tell us your nightmares and fantasies.

Had the killer not been satisfied by his fantasies inside the club and decided to act them out in real life?

His gaze slid from Theo to the victim and back again.

"Molly was a substitute for Theo." He muttered under his breath.

"Talking to yourself again, lad?"

Max snorted and glanced over at his Superintendent. "I needed expert advice, Mike. Who the fuck am I gonna talk to that's as good as me."

Mike chuckled, the grey whiskers of his mustache twitching. "I keep expecting to walk in here and find that you've gotten humble in your old age, Max."

"Then you'll know I'm an imposter and to put a bullet in my head."

Max turned back to the board. He felt Mike come to stand beside him.

"Tell me whatcha see, Max."

Max scanned the photos, putting the pieces together in his head before he started to tell Mike his theory. "The victim was killed for how similar in looks she is to one of the owners of The Player's Lounge, Theodora Caden. Hair is dyed the same colour. Eyes are different. Similar height and build. Is it a warning or a substitute? When will the fantasy not be enough?"

Taking a second, Max walked over and touched the picture of the first victim, Mark Shaw. "Security guard who worked at the club. I did some digging last night and one of the staff told me that Shaw and the other partner of the club, Kaan Sydin, hooked up frequently."

Mike lifted his busy brows. "Disgruntled employee? Or lover?"

"Molly had a boyfriend. He has an alibi. Was at a conference in Dublin when the murder happened. Though nothing to disprove your theory but my gut tells me that the killer is targeting people who worked at The Player's Lounge."

Mike clasped him on the shoulder. "I trust your gut. Tell me more, lad."

"I think all the answers we need are inside the walls of the club, but there is no way anyone at the club is going to let us see beyond the public perception that it is just a nightclub."

"You might have to just delegate and send someone in undercover."

Max snorted, shaking his head. "If you want a job done right, you gotta do it yourself. If my face wasn't splashed all over the papers, I could do it myself."

"The joys of being a hero, Max. Keep me updated with anything you find. And try not to scare any more newbies. I heard you nearly made Garda Dillion wet herself at the crime scene."

Max had to think to remember who Mike was talking about, then he realized it was the newbie Max had thought was gonna vomit all over the crime scene. "Huh, thought she'd have quit already. But if you don't want me upsetting the fresh meat, Mike, then don't send rookies who haven't seen a dead body to my crime scenes."

Mike was laughing as he left Max alone in the incident room. Max picked up the file that someone had compiled about Theo Caden. She was a dual citizen of Ireland and Romania, where her family had originally come from. She was twenty-five years old according to her date of birth. He glanced at the court documents that had a redacted amount of inheritance that Ms. Caden had revived upon the death of her father a few years back.

There were no details of her father or her mother. It appeared as if Theo had attended a private boarding school, much like Max had done. It wasn't a place Max had heard of before and when Max looked it up online, the place had been closed for a number of years.

He had the information about properties that Theo and Kaan owned together. Looked like they had their fingers in a few different pies, including a monthly sizable donation to a women's refuge in London.

But what made Max suspicious was that he couldn't find any

of the mundane things that people had. Theo, Kaan, and a few more of The Player's Lounge employees had no medical or dental records. No hospital visits. Not dental check-ups. Not even a speeding ticket. Everyone went to the doctors as a kid. Everyone got sick.

Max himself had rarely been ill but even he'd gone for regular check-ups with his GP. Shauna had been more prone to illness, he remembered her being in hospital for a week with an infection. But there were only a handful of employees of the club that had notable records.

Looking deeper into the employees and the club, Max realized that all of the suspects that had little or no details available about their past, all had the same address; a house owned by Theo Caden and Kaan Sydin.

The door to the incident room opened and in walked Rían, a file in his hand.

"Autopsy report." He said as he handed off the file to Max.

"You always bring me the best presents." Max retorted, as he opened the file.

"Only you would think an autopsy report is a gift, Max."

Max ignored him as she ran his eyes over the report.

"Just like the first victim, Molly was assaulted with a blunt instrument. I found splinters."

Rían didn't have to mention where he had found the splinters Max had already suspected considering that Mark Shaw had splinters in his rectum when his body was autopsied. Max noted that Rían had found a fracture in the girl's skull and deduced it had happened before she hit the concrete.

"What about the DNA from under her fingernails?"

Rían leaned a hip against the table. "Too neat to have happened during a struggle. I think the killer did it postmortem. The neatness of it. They had to have time to do it."

"You get a match in that fancy database of yours?" Max asked, not taking his eyes off the report.

"Nope. Unfortunately. Though I did manage to isolate the sample enough to tell you that the DNA is female. And not the victim's."

Max lifted his gaze and arched a brow. "Any chance we have a prior hit on any of the female employees of The Player's Lounge?"

Rían gave a shake of his head. "Nada. I might not be a hero Detective like you but even I found it strange that a club with so many rumours about what goes on there, isn't in any database."

Max ignored Rían's teasing and flipped over the page, reading the first few lines before he said to Rían, "You found saliva on the puncture wounds on her neck."

Rían closed his eyes, and Max gave him a minute. For all their back and forth, Max understood that Rían was far less able to compartmentalize then Max was. And he spent more time with the victims than Max ever did.

When Rían opened his eyes again, Max could see a quiet determination in them. "No match in the system but it's defo male DNA. Which also adds to my hypothesis that the DNA under the fingernails was planted."

"I think we need a warrant to take DNA samples from everyone at the club. Did you figure out what kind of instrument could be used to pierce the skin like that?"

Rían ran a hand through his blond locks. "Don't tell me I'm mad because I have scientific evidence to back it up, but it was teeth."

Max gave his friend a skeptical look, even as memories tried to claw him down into the dark. "Are you trying to convince me that a human had teeth sharp enough to pierce through flesh?"

"There is a whole subculture of people who have gotten implants or sharpened their teeth to appear like vampires. I know you aren't exactly on board with the vampire genre considering, but it is a thing. And from my findings, I can't find any way to dispute that someone with fangs bit our poor Molly."

Considering...

Rían's polite way to reminding Max that his mam had thought his dad was a vampire.

Not that Max could ever forget.

"So, say I believe you." Max ventured, continuing to scan the report. "That some fella is walking round Cork with sharpened fangs biting people. There would be more victims, right? And Shaw didn't have any bite marks on his neck."

"No, but he had them in a more...delicate place." Rían said with a wince. "Body hadn't been released yet so I went back and examined it. I found the same marks at the veins by his scrotum."

"Was blood taken? From either victim?"

"Hard to tell because they lost so much blood from other wounds. But there was a trickle of blood on Molly's neck. I found saliva on Shaw too, might indicate the killer licked the blood."

Max could see that Rían had paled a little more, and as Max wasn't the warm and fuzzy kind of guy, he closed the report and set it down on the table with the other files as he went to write the details on his board.

"I'd murder a nice steak right now. A nice, rare steak."

Max glanced at Rían who was glaring at him. "You are such an asshole."

Max just chuckled, went back to his board.

"You might be interested that The Player's Lounge holds a vampire themed night at least once a month."

Max turned to Rían. "How'd you find that out?"

Rían grinned, that smug smile of his already telling Max that he'd gotten it from a woman. "You remember that tattoo artist I dated a few times?"

"Dated is a different word than I would use, Rían." Max said drily, as Rían just grinned.

"Well, whatever. She had the whole goth girl thing going on and wanted to fuck me because of my job. She invited me to one of those nights at The Player's Lounge. It was wild. She gave me some punch that tasted like it had blood in it."

Well, that was an interesting snippet of news. Not Rían and his numerous lovers. But the fact that The Player's Lounge hosted a vampire night and a killer who was pretending to be a vampire had killed right on the doorstep of said club.

"Before you say anything, there is no way they are gonna let a known Garda into the club with all the things that go down on nights like that. Everything is fairly legal, Max, but not entirely vanilla."

Max didn't care what consenting adults got up to once no one was underage or forced to participate. He didn't care if the club was re-enacting some vampire fanfiction like they were filming for Passionflix, but if the killer had some kind of vampire fetish, then it would stand to reason that the next time that there was a vampire night, the killer would be there, hunting its next victim.

Max closed his eyes. His blood sang in his veins. It was like he had the killer already in his sights and he wanted to become the hunter instead. His entire body felt like it was on fire.

"Max, you okay? You look a bit flushed."

Rían's voice broke through his deranged thoughts. Max took a deep breath, then offered his friend what passed for a smile with him. "I'm grand. Looks like I might have to go and speak to the owners of the club again. See if any of their regular patrons through up any red flags. Unless you want to give that tattoo artist a call and see if she can get us into the club without me playing nice with my top suspects?"

"Fuck no," Rían barked out, shaking his head, the blond waves shifting with the movement. "I knew she was into kinky shit, but she wanted me to fuck her on an autopsy table. For me to pretend she was a murder victim. I'm not opposed to a bit of role play, but even that was a bit too far for me."

Max laughed. See this is why he didn't date. People were strange, fucked up creatures.

"I guess you are going to have to go and pretend to be charming with the owners of the club now, won't you?"

Max swore aloud and that had Rían bent over with laughter.

He didn't know how to be charming; he was blunt and abrasive. He couldn't fake sincerity, especially with people who were the ones at the top of his suspect pool. But he had a murderer to catch, and he needed inside that club.

His blood began to sing again, and Max liked how it made him feel.

# THEO

After a restless few hours of tossing and turning, and a cat who decided it was totally acceptable to jump on the bed and complain about how fucking pampered he was. Louis whined and whined until Theo had rolled over and then he hissed in her face and sauntered off the bed and out the door. Theo got up and decided she needed to take out her frustration with a good, sweaty, sparring session.

Well, once she cleaned up the cat vomit that she stepped in on her way to the bathroom.

See, asshole fucking cat.

Dressing in leggings and a sports bra, Theo beat her fist on Kaan's door. "Get your lazy ass out of bed and meet me in the gym."

Theo heard Kaan tell her to fuck off but knew her best friend would haul himself out of his nice comfy bed and silk sheets. Theo had done the same for him over the centuries. Their lives within the Order of the Dragon had not been a bed of roses.

It had always seemed strange to Theo that the chapter that she was raised in had chosen to raise her and Kaan together. Their parents were at war. It was Theo's job to ensure her father stayed alive and Kaan's to do the same for his. They trained together. They bunked together. They ate together.

Like it or not, a bond was inevitable.

All children who are given to the Order of the Dragon, spend their first few years living with those loyal to their respective monarchs. Theo had been taken from the Castelul Bran by her mentor Valerian Dascalu. Valerian had been hand-picked to be the one to train Theo, though he had never divulged who had chosen him to Theo.

For many years, Theo thought that Valerian was her father. When she asked him that once, he had laughed and explained to Theo who she was, what she was. Her training had started the very next night; however, it was clear to Theo that Valerian had been training her since the moment she could stand on her own.

As a Velesan, Valerian had the ability to wield any weapon with expertise once that weapon had been touched by someone else. He used that knowledge to train Theo, then Kaan and a few other children who passed through the Order of the Dragon.

They had other teachers...but that was not a path Theo wanted to think about right now.

Those ghosts always came to haunt Theo...especially since those ghosts had been hunting her for a very long time.

Shaking her head to clear those thoughts from her mind, Theo headed down the main stairs, then nodded in greeting to some of the vampires who went about their tasks. They had all sought her permission and protection to stay in Cork, and in turn Theo had given them all roles within the Scion.

The gym was situated at the back of the estate, with trees and forestry shielding it from outside view. Not that a mere human would be able to sneak onto the property. The gentle giant that was Silas, who looked more Viking than his Russian heritage, was more paranoid about security than any of them and he ran a tight ship.

Silas had been made a vampire after shoving Kaan aside during a skirmish in Europe and taking a blade meant for Kaan. That immediately made him part of the family. Though Theo did think that if Kaan had known how Silas' powers would manifest, then he might have reconsidered.

The sun affected him in a strange way that none of them understood too well. When standing in direct sunlight, Silas' molecules fused together, making his skin impenetrable. That sounded like an awesome power to have but in the beginning, his nerves would be in constant pain.

Silas learned to deal with the pain, but Theo knew that when he needed to recharge, the pain was excruciating. It also meant that when he was fully charged as he called it, he couldn't feel touch. And when his reserve was low, even the barest of touches felt like a million bee stings.

Theo and Kaan had never been able to figure out if the pain Silas felt was all in his head, like when someone gets a pain in a phantom limb, or not. They were always careful not to touch Silas unless he initiated it first.

There was only one vampire who Silas allowed to touch him no matter what status his powers were at.

Emery Charles was a Zayan, reborn through Blair after Theo and Blair had been in London and heard rumours of a vampire keeping humans in cages for vampires to feed on and rape. Theo had sliced the head of the madam running the brothel clean off, and every vampire that was on the madam's books.

Many of the humans had one foot in the grave already, so they had been granted a merciful death. Others were taken to a refuge. Emery had come home with them. Blair had found her first, beaten and broken sitting on a swing in a cage, a dead human under her feet.

Emery had been humming, sounding like birds on a spring morning. She looked childlike, and that had made Theo sick to her stomach, knowing that was exactly why she was in this horrible place. She looked up at them, tilted her head, then as Theo had seen madness in her pale green eyes, decided to end her suffering, the woman said. "He told me you would come. The Night Lord. He said your name when he was inside me."

She had collapsed then, death coming for her, and Blair had glanced at Theo, who just nodded. Blair turned Emery into a vampire because if Theo had done it, then her death would have only been delayed. The Night Lord that Emery had spoken of was one of the mentors who hunted Theo and her Scion. There was a reason she had not made a Zayan in a very long time.

There was only one remaining Zayan made by Theo walking this world.

The rest had all been murdered.

It had been Silas who had offered to carry the newly made

vampire when she was too weak to stand on her own two feet, who had helped her feed from a human the first time, even though technically is should have been Blair, despite the physical cost to him in pain.

Emery was sat with her knees to her chest, looking out the window at the birds in the trees. When they had first moved in here and Emery had taken to this corner to look out at the birds, Silas had built her a little seat in an alcove. It had also been the first windows that were built to keep out the sun.

Theo walked over to stand beside her, gently touching her hand to the top of Emery's head. Her blond hair was hung in loose curls. While Emery looked barely of legal age, she had been in her twenties when the madam had put her to work.

"I do not like the winter. The birds do not sing as much." Her voice was lyrical, a song in every word she spoke. Blair had the ability to mesmerise like a cobra, holding her prey with her eyes so she could kill them. Blair's downside was that she had to keep eye contact and that left her open to being attacked herself.

Emery could mesmerise by humming. Sometimes, when her trauma crept up to hold her hostage, Emery would rock back and forth and hum, holding them all in her grasp. Theo hated the way it made her feel, but the girl was not to blame for what happened to her.

"Silas told you he would build you an aviary." Theo said as she stroked Emery's hair.

"No." Emery replied as she shook her head. "I know what it is like to be trapped in a cage."

"You will never be in a cage again, Emery. On my life."

Emery looked up at her. "I know. A cage is just a pretty prison, Theo. Do not let them close the door on you."

Theo wanted to ask Emery what she meant but there was no point. Sometimes, Emery spoke in riddles and made little sense. She left the vampire to her own devices and went out into the gym. The space had a wooden floor, with equipment all around for the Velesan and Zayan to use. There was also a wall at the back of the space that held a variety of weapons for everyone to train with.

Theo stretched her limbs and once she felt she was good to go, she picked up one of the sticks on the wall and began to practice her strikes. The familiarity of it sank into her bones, reminding her of how she started her training, and the first time she had met Kaan.

Theo grunted as she brought the stick down in a cutting arch for what must have been the five hundredth time. Every time the Valerian calmly said again, Theo wanted to ram the stick right through his chest. Theo knew that as her mentor, and High Trainer of the Order of the Dragon, she should be respectful of him, grateful that she had such an experienced trainer as her mentor, but she had been practising with this blasted stick since the sun had set, with no end in sight.

"Again, Theo."

Theo grumbled a curse under her breath, sweat slick on her skin. But she kept up the respective action, even as her arms burned, and her legs began to shake.

"Stop."

The order came out in a harsh tone causing Theo to freeze and almost drop her stick. Straightening. Theo held the stick close to her chest as she looked up at Valerian. The Velesan had hair of silver, with piercing blue eyes. He was broad and muscular, filling out the black pants and tunic he wore when training her.

Theo glanced away from Valerian toward the footsteps that came down the hallway of the cave. A woman with a stern face and olive skin pushed a boy in front of her. It was hard for Theo to figure out how old he was, because Velesan aged differently. Besides, birthdays were a frivolity, Valerian said. Theo only knew that she was nearing a decade old because she had overheard it mentioned by the trainers.

This boy seemed to be about the same age as she was.

The woman shoved the boy forward, inclined her head to Valerian, then swept from the room without a second glance. It didn't escape her notice that the boy looked relieved to be away from the woman.

It had been a while since Theo had any company in the Order of the Dragon. When she had arrived, with Valerian, the others had been older, had been about to embark on the missions that had brought them here to be trained.

For too long now, the only person Theo had to talk to was Valerian.

"Theo, come."

Setting aside her stick, Theo strode over and stood before the boy. He had sun-kissed skin and dark locks that made Theo imme-diately jealous. Her own skin was pale, and her hair a mousy brown that was mostly tangled.. The boy looked like he could sweep a hand through it, and it would be silky to the touch.

His lips were pressed in a firm line, and Theo had to tilt her head to look at him. She was used to being shorter than the fully grown Velesan who came by from time to time, but it only reminded Theo of her weaknesses.

"Theo, this is Kaan. He will start his training to ensure his Ottoman's safety with us tonight."

Theo narrowed her gaze. The Ottomans were her father's enemies. Why the hell would Valerian want them training together? One day, Theo might have to fight this boy to keep her father safe, and likewise for the boy.

"Kaan, this is Theo. She is the Paza for the Voivode."

The boy, Kaan, narrowed his dark eyes at her. Theo almost smiled as she suspected that Kaan had thought the exact same thing as her. They were born to be immortal enemies. There was no sane reason as to why they would be trained together.

"Time to show Kaan what he will be learning to do, Theo. No powers."

Theo heard a cackle of laughter as she turned, swallowing hard as she came face to face with the nightmare twins. Eris and Keres, Greek Goddesses cursed by Zeus to become Velesan, though they were not birthed, simple created by gods, came in to face her.

Theo stepped back, and instantly regretted it as Eris, who fed on fear, licked her lips. She had no time to argue with Valerian, who had stepped aside. Theo only had a fleeting moment to shove the boy aside and face the brunt of the twins. Theo might have been a powerful Velesan, but the twins had the ichor of Gods running in their veins.

If the display was to show Kaan how much he would have to learn, the moment Keres, who fed on pain, gripped Theo's head and squeezed, causing her to black out, should have been enough.

Hours later, when Theo woke in her cot, it was to the boy Kaan cleaning her face with a damp cloth. Their eyes met and in them, an understanding passed between them. Destiny might have meant that they would be enemies, but in that moment, they had chosen to be allies.

Over time, they became friends, and then family.

"Oh no, you're thinking about the past again."

Theo opened her eyes to see Kaan lingering in the doorway of the gym. He wore loose workout pants and a sleeveless vest. Theo smiled sheepishly, standing in a resting stance before she offered Kaan a response.

"I was remembering the first time we met."

"You wanted to kill me. I could see it in your eyes."

Theo grinned, a warmth in her chest. "Then you were kind to me. I'm not sure when you stopped being kind and became an asshole though."

Kaan barked out a laugh as he strode over to Theo, confidence in his stride. "About the time that you became a dried-up old hag, darling. You know if you indulged every now and then, maybe you wouldn't be dragging me from bed to release the tension."

Theo arched a brow, then walked over to put down her stick. "Considering I know for a fact that you haven't had sex in a while either, brother, because you and a certain hustler are dancing round one another, you cannot lecture me on my sex life."

Kaan growled and that made Theo laugh. Her friend wasted no time in attacking her, immediately putting Theo on the defensive. She dodged the strike even as Kaan circled for another attempt forcing Theo to quickly raise her hands in self-defence. Kaan smirked, and Theo felt her adrenaline surge as she ducked low, shifting her weight as she angled herself and kicked out, barely missing Kaan's crotch.

"That is literally the definition of a low blow," Kaan

muttered as he looked down as if to double check everything was intact.

"I'm sorry," Theo replied holding back a laugh even as she continued, "What part of take any advantage did YOU forget?"

The air positively crackled with tension as the muscle in Kaan's jaw twitched, the only indicator that he was about to put an end to this sparing almost as quickly as it had begun. There was no way Theo was about to hand him any kind of victory as her mind raced to try and come up with a plan.

Before Kaan could attack again, Theo closed her eyes and called her power to her. Unlike her father, she had not inherited his ability to wield fire, instead Theo had inherited the ability to astral project her body. Once Theo had mastered it, Theo had used it to her advantage. But like all powers, there was a pitfall. Her astral self could be hurt, and the wounds reflected on Theo's true self. And while her astral self was active, Theo was immobile unable to withstand an attack.

Her astral self appeared behind Kaan and kicked him right in his ass, sending him flying forward. Kaan growled and lifted his hands. The light sucked from the room, leaving Theo cursing in the dark. Her astral self snapped back into her and then the light that Kaan let loose on the room made her eyes water and Theo couldn't move.

A leg swept under her feet and Theo blindly grabbed for Kaan, the two of them falling to the floor. Kaan cut off his power as they lay side by side on the ground, panting.

Theo held up her fist and Kaan bumped it.

"We really need to get laid if this is the most fun we've had in a while." Kaan drawled and he just laughed when Theo punched him in the arm.

"Maybe if you stop pushing a certain Zayan away, then you might have better fun than this."

Kaan didn't say anything, and they just lay there, getting their breath back.

"Is it him, do you think? The murders?" Kaan asked Theo, shifting so that their shoulders touched.

"I hope not," Theo admitted, resting her hands on her stomach. "I like it here. I don't wanna run again."

"Then we don't run. We stay and fight. We have lived a very long time, Theo. We were born to fight for a cause that wasn't ours to begin with. It would be an honour to die fighting for something that was truly ours."

No more words were needed. They would fight. If the nightmares had come to take from them again, they would stand and fight.

MAX

Max had intended to go to The Player's Lounge to ask Theo and the staff more questions right after he clocked in for his shift, but it seemed the universe had other plans for him. He got the call as he drove toward the station, turned on his flashing lights and did a U-turn in the middle of the road, glaring at the stupid people who blasted their horns at him.

He drove out into the countryside, up a road that would never be classed as a road anywhere else but Ireland, the tiny slip of concrete parted in the middle by a strip of grass. Max could see the flashing lights in the distance, stopping only to flash his badge at the uniforms standing in the rain and cold to stop reporters or nosy pricks from coming up the road.

Parking his car in the first available spot, Max got out just as two Garda came out of the house dressed in white crime scene suits, and vomited in the grass at the side of the house. He rolled his eyes, striding forward as his boss came out of the house dressed in one of those white all in one suits and pulled off his gloves.

One look at the blanched skin of his boss let him know it must be a really bad scene.

Mike looked over and spotted Max heading for the house. When Max went to stride right on into the house, Mike put a hand against his chest, thankfully the one without the bloody glove on.

"You're gonna want a white suit, lad. Besides, that young fella in there already said that you were not allowed to walk around his crime scene without proper duds."

Max rolled his eyes again. He hated the fucking white suit, it felt too constraining, like it kept him from getting a feel for the scene. But if Rían was adamant that he needed to wear the suit, Max would wear the suit.

Mike handed him a suit and some booties, and Max quickly slipped it on, leaving the hood down. He was offered something to put under his nose to negate the smell in the house, but Max needed his nose as much as he needed his other senses.

That strange feeling of being watched caused the hairs on his neck to stand and Max glanced over his shoulder and into the darkness. There was this moment, an insane one, where Max felt like he was staring right at whatever was out in the night, his stomach clenching.

Pushing the feeling aside, Max turned his attention back on the house. There was only one road that would take you to the property, and the nearest house was a couple of miles away. The person who lived here obviously wanted their privacy. It was far enough from the main road to Mallow, a town just outside Cork City, that you'd never expect to find it out here.

Whoever had come with the intention of killing tonight had to have known the person or people in the house, and known that they would be in. Max hadn't seen any cars that might belong to the deceased but there had been too much of a presence in the front of the house for him to really narrow down any vehicles.

Max stepped over the threshold, and immediately the scent of blood and decay invaded his senses, the scents so strong that Max knew he should be as sickened by it as the others. The problem was that he wasn't. Shit like this didn't bother him and his therapist put it down to an overactive need to compartmentalize due to the trauma inflicted from witnessing his dad's murder.

The hallway and probably beyond looked like something from a slasher movie. Blood soaked the carpet, giving it a brown sort of colouring instead of the yellow that was dotted on clearer areas.

There were streaks of blood and gore all along the walls, and one of the techs was taking a picture of what looked like fingerprints on the wall. If this was the same killer that they were already looking far, Max suspected that any bloody fingerprints would not lead to anything useful.

The blue booties were already bloody as Max glanced into the living room. There was a lot more blood than out in the hallway. Blood streaked the carpet, like a body was possibly dragged along the ground. Stepping inside the room, Max glanced down to see a bloody limb lying on the ground.

His eyes scanned the room. Furniture was ripped to shreds by what looked like animal claws, and blood stained the couch, and the armchairs. There was more blood on the walls, as well as pieces of flesh and bone. Max heard someone gag, and immediately shouted at them to get the fuck out. The last thing he needed was someone contaminating what was already a huge mess of a crime scene.

Now alone in the room, he slowly ran his gaze toward the corner. The naked body of a young man in maybe his twenties was slumped against the wall, his eyes wide in fear and even more haunting as the opaqueness of death had settled over them. The young man's body had been clawed to ribbons; Max could see bone through the jagged wounds. He was missing an arm, so Max concluded the limb he had seen in the doorway belonged to the man. His heart was also missing from his chest.

Max could tell that some of the blood had genuinely come from the dead man, but it occurred to him that some of the blood had to have been thrown at the man's body, like a painter flinging paint at a canvas. The patterns were all wrong.

Crouching down in front of the man, Max leaned over the man to get a closer look at his neck. Sure enough, there was bite marks on the man's neck, but they looked like older marks. Was this man one of the people who frequented The Player's Lounge vampire night?

Max would need to have the body washed to see if he had any other bite marks, even though he already felt certain that the blood was masking other marks.

Rising to his feet, Max took one last look around to room to ensure that he hadn't missed anything before walking back into the hall. He heard the baritone of Rían's voice, singing to himself down the hallway and he knew that his friend only did that when a scene was particularly hard for him to process.

As he passed through the hallway, he spared a glance into one of the bedrooms, saw maybe two more victims in a similar pose as the man in the living room. The blood and gore that was meant to shock a person was evident throughout, but as Max counted the number of victims, he was starting to piece things together.

"His brain works differently to the rest of us. He thinks with the mind of a killer. Thank fuck he works for us."

Max stopped dead. Why would that be the thought that punched through his mind on a night like this? He could over analyse it all or he could get on with the job.

He saw an orange marker on the ground and bent down to exam what turned out to be an organ. There was no doubt that it was a human heart, the tear on the vessels sloppy, like it was ripped clean out of one of the victim's chests. What Max was drawn to were the puncture wounds at the centre of the heart. It looked like there was no blood left in the organ at all, and it was discarded like it was nothing in the hallway.

Max left Rían alone for a few more minutes and went into the small kitchen. The chairs had been thrown against the walls; some lay in smithereens on the ground. It dragged him back to his own past, the memories still raw in his mind after his nightmare.

There was a wildness in her eyes that Max had never seen before. Her hair was dishevelled, and her clothing torn. She had blood dripping down her arms and a cut to her face. The only way that Max could describe her face was feral.

Her features softened when she looked at him. She leaned back, then jumped to her feet with a grace that surprised Max into taking a step back.

"Max, my love." She started, sounding like his mam but he was struggling to believe what he had just seen. His mother had murdered his father. His father was lying dead on the floor.

"You felt it, didn't you?" She continued, that creepy smile

curving her lips. "You felt it in your bones and came home. My son. My legacy. It's in our blood."

Max shoved down the memory and focused on the body of the young woman on the floor in front of him. The blood that surrounded her was her own, Max believed, the way her body had been sliced seemed to be to inflict as much pain as possible. Her wrists were cut, then there was a longer cut right in the centre of her forearms.

There was a long gash to the woman's abdomen, that would have been made with a slim blade. Max considered that it looked like a fingernail was dragged around the skin but while nails could cut someone, they couldn't cut as deep as the wound was. Her body looked like it had been painted in her own blood, but Max concentrated on the area in which blood was missing.

Like the killer had deliberately left no blood there.

Teeth marks that had not pierced the flesh ran from the inside of the woman's thighs right up to her pelvic area. Rían was the medical expert but to Max, the bites looked different in size, like the bites were inflicted by several different people.

The woman's head had been bashed against the ground, and the blood then soaked into her hair. It wouldn't surprise Max if the killer or killers had rubbed the blood into her hair so that it had that reddish brown taint to it.

The singing stopped down the hall.

Max looked over at the kitchen table. Kitchen knives of all sizes and blades were lined up on the table. Not even one of them looked clean or unused. The once white tablecloth was stained with blood, so much so that it dripped down onto the floor adding to the carnage.

Leaving the kitchen, Max headed down to the last bedroom at the back of the house. Stepping over the threshold, he felt his feet squelching in the bloody carpet. This was where the murderer had paid the most attention. This room was the master-piece, and the real focus of all his rage.

Unlike the other rooms, there wasn't just one victim in the bedroom but multiple. A massive bed in the centre of the room, the sheets soaked in flesh and blood. The bodies looked staged, like the four people in the bed had been engaged in a sexual act, their bodies looked like they were still joined.

A fifth victim was sat on a chair facing the bed, like he was watching what was happening on the bed. But instead of a look of pleasure on his face, Max only saw fear. The naked man on the chair had one hand on his flaccid cock, in the other hand which rested on his thigh held a heart clutched in it.

Max didn't look at Rían yet, his friend examining the bodies on the bed, but remained silent as he took in the angles of the four bodies on the bed. Two men and two women. One of the males had his face buried between the legs of one of the women, while the second male was kneeling behind him, his hand on the nape of the first man's neck which has blood dripping down from a large slash.

There were bite marks on the ass of the second man, as well as cuts on the back of the man's calves. It wouldn't surprise Max if they found more cuts in places most likely to bleed heavily.

The second female victim on the bed lay on her back, her eyes staring at the ceiling with the leg of a chair in her grasp and it thrust between her legs. A blood-coated hand lay on her breast which belonged to the first woman with the man's head between her legs.

It was then Max knew that the monster they were hunting for Molly's murder was the same person who had laid waste to those in this house.

"Their bodies are in full rigor. I'm almost positive they were already dead when the fucking sadist posed them."

That would have been a small mercy to the victims, though Max was certain that before died, that they would have suffered terribly.

"It's messy." Max finally said, causing Rían to glance at him. "Although parts feel the same it's lacking the efficiency we've seen with the hostess and the security guard. This looks like the killer wanted to glut themselves on the kill. This is personal. He wanted them found like this to demean them. I think this was the first kill."

"Looks like it." Rían answered in a solemn tone. "I've never seen anything like this before, but this looks like he or she couldn't help themselves."

Max thought the same thing. The killer had been thinking about this for a long time. It excited him. Max was certain it was a man. Felt it in his marrow that they were looking for a man or men. Someone who was angry, and this made him feel powerful.

Max glanced at the other man sitting in the chair watching. Had the killer sat on the chair while they all had sex? Had the thoughts of what he was going to do made him excited? Or had he joined in?

No.

Max decided that this killer was angry because he felt over-looked. He felt excluded from all the fun, and this was his revenge. Walking over to the man in the chair, he looked at the heart in the third man's hand.

"You done with him?" Max asked Rían and his friend nodded.

"Can't do much more now until I get them on my table."

Mike came into the room as Max reached toward them and picked up the heart. It was heavy, with no evidence of any bites on it. He gave it a squeeze and blood squirted out. Mike looked like he was going to get sick.

"The heart isn't human." Max told the other men in the room. "A human heart weighs between seven and 15 ounces. I'd bet that this is a cow's heart. A cow heart can weigh up to five pounds. That's the only way to tell them apart. The weight."

"They found a cool box thrown into the bushes on the way down the road that had lots of organs in it. I'm hoping to God that it's animal and not human." Mike said, then he asked Rían if they were ready to remove the bodies.

Rían gave a sharp nod of his head. "I'll go organise the vans."

Mike waited until Rían had left before he turned his attention on Max. "Right, lad. Do your thing...tell me what happened here."

Max closed his eyes and played out the scene in his head before he began to speak. "He hit this room last, knowing they were probably distracted and not paying attention to what was going on around the house."

"There was music blaring in the room when the uniforms did a welfare check." Mike said, then closed his mouth to let Max continue.

"The blood in the hallway is gonna be a mix of human and animal. There's too much of it for the bodies. This was designed to have maximum impact. He wanted whoever was to find this place to walk in and be completely shocked. He killed the man in the front room first but took the heart later. He originally planned to just throw the animal hearts around the gaff, but at some point he felt compelled to make it more real."

Max glanced out the door toward the kitchen. "He took his time with the woman in the kitchen. He enjoyed inflicting pain. The victims in the first bedroom looked quick, like they were not who he was after. Then he moved on to the main bedroom."

Max closed his eyes and imagined the killer striding into the room. "He had some way of keeping the men subdued and willing to do what he told them to. The men are muscular, look like they could defend themselves, but they didn't. He toyed with them until his need for blood overwhelmed him. He took his time to pose them, to embarrass them. He was strong enough to do it too... posing a dead body is not easy. He then went about making the scene look ever gorier, like he'd watched too many B movie horrors."

"He then went back to the kitchen and practised on the dead woman. I think he cut the victim in the living room's heart out next and then for some reason, he bit it, then drank the blood like it was a Capri Sun."

Max opened his eyes to see Mike hold a hand to his mouth, but his eyes never left Max as he walked to the head of the bed and saw a streak of blood on the wall behind the door. He went back over and waited until Mike had shifted from the doorway before he closed the door.

"And he liked the way the killing made him powerful. He's addicted to it now. Knows he must be smarter. There are more bodies between this and the security guard, we just haven't found them yet. He wasn't ready to show us. Now he is."

They both looked at the words written in blood on the wall.

Only the dead have seen the end of the war.

"He's only just getting started. If he's quoting Plato about war, then he sees this as his personal war against the person all of these victims are a substitute for." Max told Mike, then asked. "Do we know which of the victims owns the house?"

Mike had a grim expression on his face. "It took a little digging. Lots and lots of digging but it came back to a company that has Theo Caden and Kaan Sydin as its CEO's."

Max snorted and looked back at the quote on the wall. The killer was preparing for war and it occurred to Max that the quote was a threat, that the only way out of this war for those who got in his way was death, and he saw himself as death in human flesh.

The case was getting more and more intense, and the blood would not stop flowing until the killer was caught. The chase was truly on...

And all roads led back to Theodora Caden.

# THEO

After showering and a quick breakfast, Theo and Kaan headed to The Player's Lounge around midday to take stock of what was going on. It would have been obvious to anyone that the murders were linked to Theo and the club, and that Detective didn't get to the position he was in by being an idiot. It would be up to Theo and the Scion to figure out who out of a long list of enemies had it in for Theo this time.

And she hoped like hell that it wasn't the vampire who wanted her dead more than most.

Silas let them in the main door, then told them that everyone was upstairs in their private suite. Once Silas had locked the door, he followed them into the lift, keeping a little distance between them. Theo and Kaan exchanged a look as their head of security even avoided leaning against the wall of the lift.

The vampire must have recharged at sunrise today and his skin must feel like it was being stabbed a zillion times over. As if he sensed her looking at him, Silas lifted his gaze to Theo's, his pale blue eyes holding hers with a taint of darkness as he said.

"Blair brought Emery in today. Said she wanted to keep an eye on her."

Theo knew that was Blair's kind way of saying that she was worried that Emery was about to lapse into one of her manic episodes where she either shut down completely and they had to force her to feed, or she left her humanity behind and drained a human when she fed. They already had enough for the Detective to be looking at...they didn't need any more bodies dropping that kept his focus on them.

"Did you manage to contact everyone who was needed at the

meeting?" Kaan asked Silas, drawing the Zayan's attention to him.

Silas grinned, the darkness in his eyes brightened. "If you are wondering if a certain smartass has returned from his spying, then yes. Only one who I couldn't reach was Carmen."

This was not unusual for Carmen, but Theo knew that the vampire would get in touch when she could.

Kaan sighed in response to Silas, which made the other vampire's grin even bigger as the elevator came to a halt. Theo arched her brow as Kaan smoothed down the front of his jacket, scowled at Theo, then strode out into the suite that Theo kept for just the Scion.

Laughter and music made Theo smile as she followed Kaan out, ensuring that she stayed well out of Silas' way. The slightest bump, the gentlest brush of fingers against his skin could cause him excruciating pain. It said a lot for his tolerance of pain that he was even upright and coherent because in the beginning, it had not been out of the ordinary for the vampire to be curled in a ball in the corner because of the pain.

"I'm fine, Theo. You don't have to worry."

Theo offered him a smile. "It's my job to worry, Silas. As Suzerain, I get to worry about all you assholes."

Silas snorted but didn't say anything else as Theo rounded the corner. Blair was sat perched on the edge of the private bar laughing at something Maisie had said. Kaan had taken a seat in one of the armchairs by the unlit fireplace, trying to look anywhere but at the vampire who lay across the bar like it was a sun lounger, throwing knifes in the air and catching them with ease, as if they were juggling balls and not deadly blades.

Emery sat in one of the corner booths, her chin on her knees as she hugged them to her chest. Maisie turned when Theo strode in, and did something on her phone to turn off the music. Silas went over to where Emery was sitting, the blonde vampire tilting her head before she scooted closer to Silas and leaned her head against his muscular arm.

Theo held her breath as a muscle ticked in Silas's face, obviously in pain, but made no attempt to move the other Zayan.

Blair reached behind her and took out a bottle of vodka and took a slug from it before she handed it off to Maisie.

"Want a drink, Theo?" Kannon asked her, halting his knife juggling to sit up in a smooth way that she had become accustomed to with the Japanese vampire.

"Sure." Theo replied with a smile as Kannon slid off the bar to get her a large glass of red wine from her collection. She watched him pour the glass and then he added dash of blood to the wine, knowing how Theo liked it.

Kannon jumped over the bar to hand Theo her glass, winked at her before he turned round to see Kaan glaring at him.

"Do I not get offered a drink?" Kaan asked his Zayan, and the handsome vampire just shrugged.

"I wasn't sure if today was a day you would ignore me or speak to me. I was awaiting your acknowledgement, oh sire of mine." Kannon's tone was taunting, bordering on insubordinate, and had it been anyone but Kannon, Kaan would have had him by the throat, his fangs bared for such a show of disrespect.

The tension in the air thickened as they glared at one another. Maisie, who was the youngest in the Scion, hissed between her teeth and took another drink from the bottle in her hand. Rolling her eyes, Theo strode over to Kaan, standing in front of him so that she blocked his view of Kannon. Handing Kaan her glass, she gave him a look that said, "Really" before turning around to see that Kannon had already gone to fix her another drink.

Those two either needed to fuck or fight soon, or Theo would have to send Kannon away for a time. He might be a smartass, but Theo was fond of him.

The conversation started up again as Theo walked around the bar and as Kannon handed her another glass, she inclined her head for him to follow her. They went out the side door, onto a balcony that overlooked the alley below.

Theo looked at the vampire as he leaned on the railings and closed his eyes, head tilted toward the sky. His black hair ruffled in the wind, giving him a windswept look that only added to his appeal. Kannon was gorgeous to look at, with a cheeky smile and eyes that were so brown they were almost black. He had full lips that Kaan had once joked while slightly tipsy looked extremely biteable.

Stubble framed his face, and his beard was trimmed to accentuate his strong jawline. He had lashes that were meant to look at you after a long night of sex. He was lean, deceptively so, because unlike Kaan who liked to wear form fitting outfits, Kannon wore clothes that made you look at him, but didn't give you the full picture.

His skin tone was a shade lighter than Kaan's and when the two of them stood together, she could understand why Maisie had once said that they were just so damned handsome, that a woman could orgasm from looking at them.

"You're undressing me with your eyes, Theo."

Kannon's tone was teasing, and Theo used her free hand to smack him in the arm. "I'm contemplating throwing you over the balcony to try and knock some sense into you."

Kannon opened his eyes and turned to look at Theo. "Just me?"

Theo snorted then took a sip from her wine. "I've known Kaan for too long to know that when he is being stubborn, that he won't back down. I had thought you might be the one who could be reasoned with. Or will I be forced to ask you to go visit Carmen so that my fucking inner circle doesn't implode?"

Kannon's face went serious. "Don't send me away, Theo. I'll try to behave. Besides, you need me around here especially if you need me to continue to traipse after a certain Detective Sergeant."

Theo wanted to tell Kannon that she knew asking him to behave was like asking him not to drink blood...it would be fucking impossible. The first time they had meet, after Kaan had made Kannon a vampire, the thief had managed to steal from Theo, right under her own nose. He still did things like that, testing himself, but now he knew that he had to give it back.

That night, Kannon had only returned her ring when he realized that Theo, despite her small stature was the most powerful vampire in the room. After she'd put him on his ass, he had looked up at her, this massive smile on his face and asked if Theo would teach him how to do what she had just done.

"I'm not gonna send you away, Kannon. Not right now. But we are smack bang in the middle of an utter shitshow and I need everyone focused. So, sort it out. Please."

Theo turned and walked back inside, rounding the corner as Kaan looked at her with a question on his face. Kannon came in behind her, hoisted himself up on the bar and leaned against the wall, and refrained from saying anything as Theo lowered herself into one of the chairs beside Kaan.

Her best friend rose off his seat, striding behind the bar with his empty glass to refill. Theo watched Kannon tense, then was taken by surprise when Kaan set a bottle of Japanese beer down beside Kannon. The Zayan looked at the Velesan who made him with a weary curiosity.

"Thanks."

"You're welcome."

It was the most pleasant that they had been to each other in weeks and Theo could see the lick of desire in Kaan's eyes as he dragged his eyes from Kannon, drained his wine, then went for a refill.

Maisie came to sit down on one of the stools. "So, Theo, did you know that your Detective has a sister who's been to a few events here with a member? She also applied for a job but when we did a background check and saw that her brother was a guard, we quickly dismissed the idea."

"What does the sister do?" Theo asked, taking a sip of her wine, felt hunger gnaw at her stomach, and shoved it down for now.

"Art and music student at the University. Lives with the brother but from what my sources tell me, Max oversees her trust fund and ensures that the sister gets enough to live on, but not enough to go too far."

"Controlling?" Theo asked, an edge in her tone. She was used to men who thought to control her, and that would just be another reason to dislike the Detective.

Maisie shook her head, then lifted her tablet from the table. "No. Far from it from what I've seen. He pays for her college from his own trust fund. He pays all the bills. Lives modestly himself and spends the most of his millions on security for the family home and his sister."

"Anything else about him?" Theo kept her tone neutral, hoping to disguise just how much she really wanted to know everything about Max De Barra.

"Not really," Maisie replied as she swiped at her tablet. "He seems like a bit of a loner. Has no social media presence at all. I found him on some pictures on his friend's social media, Rían Kelly, who has been here a few times. They went to school together and now they work together, though Rían is a forensic pathologist. Max was engaged once to a socialite but that didn't last."

"From the way he was dressed, I cannot see Detective De Barra feeling at home on a red carpet." Kaan drawled, glancing at Theo.

"One of the gossip sites I found with a whole thread about the couple said that Max broke off the engagement amid cheating rumours and one said he was iffy about settling down. That he was married to his job."

See, to Theo that made sense. For better or for worse, she was the leader of this dysfunctional family, and that left little time for a relationship. If you slept with a man for long enough, they mostly started to talk of the future.

Any man she decided she might like to keep around for longer than a few nights would become a target. Vampire or human, it didn't matter. They would end up dead.

"Kannon, how about you tell us what you found out following the Detective."

The sound of Kaan's deep tone shook her from her memories. Before Kannon could start to speak, Theo heard Silas grunt, and they all looked over at him. It always took Theo by surprise to see the hulking vampire and the petite vampire next to one another. While they had been talking, Emery had climbed into Silas' lap, and cuddled into him, resting her head on his chest.

Blair went to push off the bar to go and collect her Zayan, but Silas shook his head.

"It's grand."

But Theo could tell from the harshness in his tone that he was far from it.

"Kannon, go on." Kaan said, then gritted his teeth. "Please."

That was enough for everyone to turn their attention to Kaan. Even Kannon was eyeing the other male with suspicion.

"Maisie's information is spot on." Kannon started, lifting his beer to his lips before he continued. "Dude goes to work, goes home, goes for a run with his dog, then tries to sleep. Looks like he has nightmares. I followed him but somehow, he knew that there was someone watching him. Hell, at times it felt like he was looking right at me."

Kaan glanced at Theo. "You didn't tell him?"

Theo shrugged shaking her head. "I didn't want to until we were sure. But I think all the evidence lines up."

Kannon narrowed his gaze. "Tell me what?"

It was Kaan that answered, like he was hoping to lessen the impact. "Max De Barra has Cathain blood in his veins."

Kannon snarled, the tips of his fangs showing. "You sent me to follow a fucking Cathainite without telling me your suspicions?"

Theo sat up a little straighter and pushed a little power in her voice as she replied. "I sent you to follow a man who has no clue as to what he is. He might have vampire hunter blood, but Max has no clue. He might have feelings and hunches, but if he doesn't know the kind of power he has under his flesh, then we are not going to educate him. And if you cannot handle yourself against one Cathainite, then perhaps I overestimated your skills."

The bottle in Kannon's hand shattered, and Theo knew she had hit a nerve because usually, it took a lot to illicit such a reaction from the Zayan. The scent of copper filled the air and it made Emery lift her head in interest for a fleeting moment before she went back to sleeping.

"I can handle myself, Theo. I just would have liked to have all the fucking information." Kannon growled. "Especially since he would have sensed me the closer I got."

"Well, now you know." She wasn't about to defend her

actions. That would only make her appear weak and weakness could get you killed.

They held each other's gazes until Kannon glanced away and then leaned over the bar to grab another drink. He drained half the bottle before he went on.

"Max got a call yesterday evening on his way to work. I followed him to the house on Mill Lane."

Theo's stomach dropped. Mill Lane was a house that she and Kaan owned on the outskirts of town that housed some of the staff who were not exactly hostesses. They were the ones who had consented to being food, both blood and sex, for vampires and they were paid handsomely for it. They liked the high that sex with a vampire gave them, and some of them were even couples who enjoyed watching their partners with vampires.

They were well looked after, in the secluded, private areas with vampire security on hand to deal with any vampires who dared breach the rules of The Player's Lounge.

"Who did we lose?" Theo asked, setting her glass down on the table.

"Everyone." Kannon said grimly.

Fuck. How the hell could this have happened? They had sent someone to check on the house.

"I texted George to check in on them and report back. I got a text back to say that everything was grand." George was the head of their human security who worked closely with Silas but looked less imposing than Silas.

"I believe that George was at the house and dead long before you texted him. He was also missing one of his arms and his heart when the guards found him."

Theo closed her eyes. "Tell me the rest."

Silence weighed down on the room, and Theo could hear her own heart beating before Kannon continued.

"I got close enough to hear the Detective assessing the scene and then the ME go through the bodies he had found, and their descriptions. Leanne was found in the kitchen. Naked. Cut to shreds. She must have gone to the kitchen for something because everyone else was killed in the main bedroom."

The people who lived in that house: Leanne, Camile, Sean, Carlos, and Adam. And all of them were now dead. Theo felt the weight of it slap her right in the face. They might have been human, but they too had been her responsibility. Their loss was her guilt to carry. Theo had seen too much death in her lifetime, had been responsible for taking a lot of lives herself, and right now, those who died felt like it had been a waste of the lives they could have had.

"The cute medical examiner said that the bodies were in full rigor, so it looks like they had been dead a few days, maybe a week. They were all off shift for two weeks while the courtesans in Bridge House worked. Someone had to know that everyone would be home." Kannon stated, hoping to ease Theo's guilt, but it didn't. Not even a little bit.

MAX

Max had followed his instincts and it had led him to another body. Having returned from the murder scene and being forced by Mike to work with the rest of the team about the killer, Max had tasked them with following reports about strange smells, neighbours who hadn't been seen in days, or anything that linked back to The Player's Lounge.

A few hours in, one of the Garda had come to him about a woman who had complained about a smell coming from one of the apartments in her building, and that the landlord was away on business so couldn't come to investigate.

The apartment was being leased to a Fallon Byrne, who worked as a bartender at The Player's Lounge. The complex was also a stone's throw from the estate where Theo and her staff seemed to live.

Max wasn't a big believer in coincidences. He relied on facts and his gut, and his gut was telling him that when he went to the apartment, sure enough he would find a dead body. He'd taken note of the address and was ready to head out when Mike had called him back.

"Take Rían with you. At least the Garda Commissioner can't give me shit for sending you off on your tod again. At least I sent the ME with ya, lad. From the look on your face you think you're going to need him anyway."

He had wanted to argue with Mike that he was only doing a welfare check, and he didn't want Rían's reactions muddying his senses, however the look on his boss's face meant that there was no way out of it. And his boss wasn't wrong. He was pretty certain he was heading to another crime scene.

His friend had been waiting for him by his car when he had gone outside, a grim expression on his face. Max pressed the button on his key to open the boot, letting Rían put his kit in there before they got in. Max started the ignition, and they barely made it out of the station before Rían started to talk.

"My mam called me yesterday and invited us to dinner."

Max snorted, knowing that there was only one reason why Aisling Kelly was inviting them both to dinner. Rían's neurosurgeon mother liked to fix him and Rían with her female students that she considered to be suitable matches for them.

The last time Aisling had invited Max to dinner, he had been so graphic with the details of a made-up case that the woman who poked and prodded in people's brains for a living had felt so ill, that she had vomited in one of the plant pots.

Max had stood and taken the lecture from Aisling with an apologetic expression, then pocketed the fifty quid he had won from Rían in the bet of who could get their date to lose interest first. If Aisling ever found out that they survived these dinners with stupid immature bets, they'd both be on her shit list.

It had always been amusing to Max that Aisling had taken Max under her wing, or at least tried to, when Aideen had been arrested, despite Max been adamant that he could look after himself and Shauna. She had realized quickly that the easiest way for Max to step out of her life, and maybe even Rían's was to try and force Max to dig his heels in.

So now Aisling just tried to set them up with women.

"I hope you told her thanks but no thanks." Max grumbled as he drove down the road.

"You have met my mother before, right? She made it clear that no wasn't an option."

Max heaved out a sigh but didn't say anything. He kept his eyes on the road and the task at hand, which was extremely difficult with a chatter box sat in the passenger side.

"I bumped into Vanessa the other night."

It wasn't the first time that Rían had brought up Vanessa, and Max knew it wasn't because he was worried that Max missed his former fiancé or was worried that Rían had actually taken

Vanessa up on her offer to warm her bed, but it was like he tried to soften any blows that might come Max's way through a reporter or social media.

Not that he had social media.

Max really couldn't be bothered with all that shite. To him, food was for eating and not taking pictures of.

When Max didn't say anything in response, Rían took that as his permission to fill Max in, when in reality, Max couldn't care less what his Ex was up to.

"Things between her and the property developer seem to be going good. She asked after ya, asked if you were seeing anyone. Then she told me herself and Shauna had lunch last week."

Max hadn't been aware that Shauna and Vanessa were still that close. They hadn't been when Max and she had been dating. When they broke up, Shauna had kept in contact with Vanessa as if to piss Max off, and she had stopped when she realized Max wasn't bothered.

Again, Max refrained from answering Rían, and heard his friend sigh before continuing with an absolutely shocking impression of him. "Oh really, Rían, that was nice of Vanessa to ask after me. I wish her the best. Christ, you can be a cold bastard sometimes, Max."

"That shouldn't be news to you, Rían."

"It's not. But every once in a while, I forget that you aren't exactly human. And not in a superhero kind of way." Rían's tone was teasing, and Max rolled his eyes, which only made his friend smile a little more.

Rain began to trickle down from above, darkening the sky, and Max immediately felt more at ease. He kept one hand on the steering wheel as he reached into the back and grabbed two bottles of water from the storage in the back.

Handing one to Rían, he opened his own bottle and took a drink. His phone chimed and he checked it to see that Shauna had arrived home with a friend midway through the school day. Rían glanced at the phone, then shook his head.

"If she ever finds out how close you watch her, she's gonna be pissed."

Max chuckled, stowing his bottle in the cup holder. "Shauna is already pissed at me for existing. If it means she's safe from the vultures wanting to make money from her trauma, I'm glad to let her continue to be pissed at me."

Rían nodded his head, then glanced to the side and looked out the window. Max noted that he looked tired, and he probably was considering all the death that had been thrown at him the last couple of days. And while Rían's job might be to look after the dead, there had not been such carnage that Rían had been forced to endure in his career.

"Do ya think we will catch them? The killer?"

"Yes." Max replied to Rían's question with a finality to his tone.

Rían turned his head to look at Max. "I wish I had your faith."

"It's not faith," Max told Rían. "It's confidence that I am that fucking good at my job that this prick will end up wearing my cuffs."

Rían barked out a laugh, and Max knew his comment had gotten the desired effect.

"What some might call confidence, others might say it's arrogance." Rían offered, still laughing.

"It's still true."

Rían was still laughing as Max parked the car outside the apartment complex. They both got out and Max locked the SUV once Rían had grabbed his kit. They walked in silence into the complex and took the elevator up to the fourth floor. The moment Max stepped out into the corridor; his senses came alive.

He knew without having to check the apartment number that there was a dead body inside the home of Fallon Byrne. He had goosebumps on his arms and anticipation in his gut. It shouldn't have been possible but while he could smell the scent of decay coming from the apartment three doors down, he also felt and scented a lot of blood.

Taking a step toward the apartment without realizing that he had moved, Max turned to Rían. "Stay out here and do not come in until I tell you. Call Mike and tell him we've got another dead body."

Rían cursed, however he didn't ask Max too many questions, just did what Max had asked him to. Max pulled a pair of gloves from the pocket of his jeans, then walked right on up to the apartment door. He knocked, identifying himself as a Garda, then twisted the handle when he got no response.

Max wasn't surprised that the door opened for him, knowing what he suspected about the killer, that they wanted their destruction to be discovered. Shoving the door open wide, Max reached for his weapon, 9mm SIG Sauer P226. Max had completed his Emergency Response Unit training that allowed him to carry a gun. He clicked the side release, preparing to fire if he was called upon.

The carpet in the hallway of the apartment was snow white, and it muffled Max's steps as he moved. He stepped into an open plan living area and saw the first drops of blood harsh against the white of the carpet. The scent of death permeated the air, but the body was not in this room.

Max moved forward; his eyes darted from side to side as his stomach twisted in pain. It reminded him of the pain he had felt when he had driven passed Erasmus Finn's house. It was the same feeling he had the last couple of days when he felt as if someone was watching him. And it was the same unease he had felt when standing in the lobby of The Player's Lounge.

A noise inside the last room at the end of the hall gave him cause to take moment. Whoever or whatever was in that room knew he was coming since he'd announced himself, so he had to be ready for whatever awaited him.

The carpet beneath his boots now was soaked in blood. Max supposed it was probably like the other house... too much blood for the dead. He was probably striding through the evidence, through animal blood, leaving his boot prints, but if the killer was in that room and Max had the chance to put a bullet between his eyes, well then he was gonna do that.

You enjoy the hunt...

He did enjoy the hunt. Max wouldn't admit it allowed but as

the voice in his head relayed his dark thoughts to him, Max quieted his mind and after a count of three, he pushed open the bedroom door and stepped into the bedroom.

Blood spatter painted the walls and the floor as Max scanned the room. He was aware that he felt utterly calm even as his heart raced with the anticipation. Pivoting so that he faced the bed, Max focused on the bed, and what was unfolding.

The body of what Max assumed was Fallon Byrne lay spread eagled on the bed, her hands and feet bound with rope to the bed posts. She was naked, a slash to her throat and blood stained her almost porcelain skin.

But that was not what Max focused on.

No, his eyes were trained on the person who straddled Ms. Byrne. They wore a black cloak that covered their face and body, and yet Max just felt that they were a woman. The woman had their face in the crook of the victim's neck and had just inhaled. They had to have heard Max enter, and yet, they didn't seem to be too bothered about his presence or the gun pointed at them.

"Armed Garda. Put your hands up and step the fuck away from the body." Max called out, a little louder than necessary so that Rían would know to stay the fuck outside. The last thing he needed was to have to try and protect Rían and end up letting the killer go.

The woman lifted her head from the dead body and inhaled again. "Your gun cannot stop me, hunter. I would feast on your pain. It has been such a long time since I have felt a hunter's heart beat for the last time in my hands."

Max's instincts told him to brace for an attack a second before the woman launched herself at Max. He hit the wall hard as he fired off a shot. The woman moved with a speed that Max didn't think a human was possible of. She smelled of violence.

His stomach clenched and a voice in his head screamed. *Vampire! Vampire!*

Lashing out, he struck the woman at the side of her head with the butt of his gun. She growled at him and dug her nails into his face as she used her other hand to smack his hand against the wall, the force of it making him loose the grip on his gun.

The gun fell to the floor and Max felt adrenaline pump in his veins. They traded blows, the woman strong as hell. They tumbled to the floor, and the woman rolled them over so that she was straddling Max's chest.

A white mask covered her face, but the woman had the blackest eyes Max had ever seen. She leaned down and inhaled, then jerked back. "No tasty morsel of fear from you, hunter. Such a shame. Such a shame."

She dug her nails into the side of his face again, dragged his head up, and then he felt pain in the back of his skull when she slammed his head onto the ground so hard that not even the softness of the carpet could soften the blow.

His vision swam and Max closed his eyes for a second.

When he opened them again, the woman was gone and Rían was shouting his name.

Rían burst into the room as Max tried to sit up, nausea rolling in his stomach as he put his hand to the back of his head, and it came away bloody. Rían forced him to stay sitting down when Max tried to rise to go after the woman.

Mike ordered him to stay where he was as Rían checked the back of his head and then looked at the claw marks on his face. He could see from the look in Rían's eyes that he was already comparing the gashes to the other victims and wondering if Max would have been the next victim.

He wasn't sure why or how he knew, but the woman wasn't the killer they were after.

"You need to go to hospital, Max."

"I'm grand." Max told his friend as he pushed his friend's hands away and got to his feet. It took him two tries, but at least he was vertical now.

"You are going to the hospital, Max, if I have to drag you there myself." Mike told him as he picked up Max's gun and handed it to one of the techs who was filing away evidence. As per protocol, because he had discharged his weapon, there would be an internal affairs check before he'd get that back.

Rían went over to check Ms. Byrne's body, then glanced over at them. "She's been dead a while. Probably shortly after the murders at the house. Very similar to the other two victims."

"Are we thinking the woman is the killer? The one who attacked Max?"

"No," Max said sternly. "Believe it or not, I think she was collecting evidence of her own. She was hunting the killer too. She definitely had some training, so maybe military or special ops? Her accent didn't sound Irish."

Mike inclined his head. "I'll check with Interpol to see if the MO is similar to any open cases in Europe." He pinned Max with a stare. "Hospital to get checked over or I swear I'll bench ya from the investigation, Lad."

Max snorted, ignoring the ache in the back of his skull. "That's an empty threat and you know it. I'm on the killer's trail, I know it. And you know it. You wouldn't bench me."

Hunter...

That was what the woman had called him. Hunter. Like it was a title. Like she had known something about him that Max didn't. There was a sense of rightness to the sound of it that left Max with too many unanswered questions, and he hated not having the answers.

Mike gave him the middle finger, then ordered that someone take Max to the hospital. As Rían ushered Max from the apartment, Max called over his shoulder that he wanted to know if they found any evidence of who the other woman was.

It was only then that Max realized that the unease in his stomach had vanished.

Maybe he was losing his mind.

He'd had all the tests to see if he would end up like his mam, had made sure they were discreetly run on Shauna too, and thankfully they had both seemed to escape the madness that had taken their mother, and in the end their father from them.

But maybe Max needed to get rechecked.

He let Rían take his keys and drive him to the hospital where they told him that he had a slight concussion as well as deep gauges to his face. They weren't sure if the scratches on his face would scar, and that a plastic surgery consult was needed.

Max had told them to fuck right off and signed himself out of the hospital. Rían drove him home, and when Max told Rían to go home, his friend had ordered food and plonked down on the sofa, telling Max that he was stuck with him for the next couple of hours to make sure his head wound didn't get any worse.

Max closed his eyes and pretended to sleep so that he wouldn't have to make small talk with Rían. He couldn't stop thinking about the woman that he had fought with, the scent of violence that seemed to radiate from her skin and how much Max had felt drawn to it.

He listened as Rían called Shauna to tell her about what had happened to him, heard Rían argue with his sister but he just tuned it all out. He ached to get back out there, looking for the killer, and sating this need inside him.

The woman had said that she didn't scent any fear from him, and she was right. He hadn't been afraid, and Max knew that should terrify him...instead it thrilled him.

THEO

"So, the killer has to be someone who knows our schedule, or could hack into our systems." Theo concluded, taking the wine glass in her hand again and taking a sip.

Maisie looked insulted as she shook her head. "There is no one who could get passed my security protocols without me knowing...not a single person."

"Might it be Landon?" Came a velvet toned voice and Theo lifted her gaze to the vampire who had been the closest thing to a real father that she had ever had.

Valerian Dascalu strode into the room with the regal air that almost betrayed his age and status. He had silver hair and blue eyes and wore a silver blazer with black pants. Valerian had broad shoulders and was muscular. As weapons master and former High Trainer of the Order of the Dragon, he had continued to stay by Theo's side when she had taken down the Order brick by brick.

He unbuttoned his jacket, smoothing down his waistcoat as he took a seat. Landon Lewis was one of the Zayan who Valerian himself had made reborn. And while Maisie had gained skills that were useful to the Scion, Landon had been pissed off that the powers he had inherited from Valerian weren't exactly useful.

The Zayan could touch an object and tell who the last person was that touched it. It might be considered useful, but if the murderer had touched something, then a Garda had, then Landon's power was useless. All powers had a downside, but at least Landon didn't taint his own power by touching an item and becoming the last person to touch it.

The Zayan had always felt hard done by because of the limitations of his powers, considering Maisie, who was younger than Landon in vampire years, had a far more significant power than Landon. It made him bitter, jealous, and ended with him deflecting to the side of their enemy.

If there was anyone who could get passed Maisie's protocols, it might be Landon.

"I'd have known if it was Landon. Every hacker has a signature, and I know Landon's as much as I know my own. There isn't anything out of the ordinary about unauthorized access to my network." Maisie told the Velesan who had sired her, that weariness in her eyes as she glared at Valerian for a hot second before she looked back at her tablet.

Theo knew that the bond between sire and Zayan could be intense. She had felt it numerous times herself when a Zayan had been reborn with her blood in their veins, knew how badly it hurt when one of them was killed. Maisie had always believed that Valerian had sired her only because he wanted to see if she would turn out like Landon. And when she didn't, he had put a massive target on her back from the aggravated Zayan.

"And what of Henry? Could he have returned to Ireland?" Valerian asked as Blair brought him a scotch.

"Henry is still in the UK." Kannon said as he went back to juggling blades.

"And how do you know that?" Kaan drawled, reclining further into his chair, resting one leg over the other.

Kannon grinned, juggling his knifes as he shrugged. "Henry doesn't hate me."

Theo rubbed her forehead. Henry was a Velesan who Theo had tried to keep a firm hold on since she and Kaan had dismantled the Order of the Dragon. He had never been happy that Theo was his Suzerain, or that she had more power than him. To be honest, she only kept him around so that he wouldn't join forces with the other side, because Henry had this warped notion that vampires were a superior race and that the Velesan should be worshipped like kings.

Funny the chauvinist never considered women worthy enough to be in power.

That surprised Theo too, considering that Henry had often made his dislike of Kaan very clear because of the fact he was gay. Henry dwelled in the time he was born in, just under four hundred years ago, and believed that he was the rightful Suzerain to the Scion based on the fact that both his parents had been Velesan.

Henry, full name Henry Tudor, or Henry IX as he liked to declare, was the Velesan son of Henry VIII and Anne Boleyn. Though many believed that Anne had miscarried the child prior to her death, including Anne herself, that child had in fact been Henry. He had been raised in the same British Order of the Dragon as Blair, though Henry had been an adult when Blair had come to train and Henry had been one of those who trained her.

Henry believed he was a king who was never crowned, that the crown that should have been his and protected the Tudor line of succession was stolen from him and as the one true born Velesan, that he should be king of all vampires.

He hated it when Theo pointed out that herself and Kaan might not have been born of two vampires, but they also had once a right to a crown that in truth, neither of them wanted.

That incensed Henry even more.

"Henry is too self-absorbed to be suitable if he finally decided to come at me. He would relish the spectacle but would want people to know it was him." Theo remarked after taking a drink of her wine, before looking over at Kaan. "You're certain he is still in England?"

Kann inclined his head. "Yup. Holed up in the place he calls his royal castle feeding and fucking. My source will let me know if that changes and you'll be the first to know."

That mollified Theo just a little. At least she knew where Henry was so if the strike was coming, she'd be prepared. Theo was about to ask Kannon for more info on what happened at the Mill Lane house when Kannon's phone rang.

A massive grin curbed the Zayan's lips as he pressed the answer button and put it on speaker before saying in perfect Spanish. "Princess Carmen, are you coming home? I have you on speaker, everyone is here."

A dark throaty chuckle sounded down the phone as Carmen replied in Japanese. "Little brother, are you still causing mischief? Giving all the men of Ireland something to lust after."

Kannon rolled his eyes even though Carmen couldn't see him before speaking in English. "I'm behaving thank you very much. Don't believe all that you hear."

Carmen laughed again and the sound of it made Theo smile. It had been years since she had seen Carmen in the flesh, because it was safer for Carmen to remain far from Theo. All of Theo's Zayan had been murdered, one by one, and Carmen was the only one who remained.

Part of that was down to Carmen's ability to slip seamlessly into a crowd and disappear. Much like Kannon, she had perfected that cat like grace. When Theo had meet Carmen, the Spanish woman had been stealing from tourists in what was now the city of Barcelona to feed her family. She'd been caught by the police and thrown in prison to be hanged.

Theo had made her an offer and Carmen had accepted it with a steely resolve.

And Theo would do anything to protect Carmen from her enemies finding out that she existed.

"Mamá, I can hear your worrying down the phone. I am all right."

Theo rolled her eyes. Carmen had Theo saved in her phone as Mamá and called her that when Theo fussed over her. It was a disarming tactic that the Zayan used all the damn time.

"I'm not worried at all, Carmen. I know you can handle yourself."

That made Carmen laugh. "I was trained by the best fighters in history."

Kannon set the phone down on the counter and asked. "You got something for me, Carmen, or did you just call because you missed us?"

"Of course I miss you idiots. Kannon, come see me soon. I have a new dagger to show you." That made Kannon grin and the rest of them groan. Kannon and Carmen were too similar to one another, and they both loved a good blade.

"I called because I got a tip off from a source to say that there was an incident this morning at the apartment of Fallon Byrne."

Fallon Byrne, real name, Diane Coughlan, was a bartender at The Player's Lounge. But she was also one of the staff who enjoyed the luxury that came with donating blood and sex to vampires. She was one of the high-end courtesan's that was sponsored by a number of wealthy vampires, and she lived a much better life than when Blair had found her working the streets as a teenager and offered her a warm bed and a job.

"Is she dead?" Blair asked.

"Sí."

Blair swore and got to her feet, walking out the door a second later to collect herself. Silas looked like he wanted to get up and go check on Blair, but Theo shook her head.

"Anything else, Carmen?"

"I believe, Mama, that your Detective Dracula was first on scene." Carmen said in teasing tone.

"For fuck sake, who told you? And he is not my Detective anything." Theo growled and that made everyone laugh.

"That growl says otherwise. But the report says that there was someone straddling the body when the Detective arrived, and they fought. He was not killed but he was taken to the hospital to be checked over."

"Was it the murderer?" Kaan asked, to which Carmen replied quickly.

"No. My spies overheard the Detective tell his boss that he didn't think the person who fought him looked like they were hunting the killer too, that she had military training or something. Then he told his friend at the hospital he didn't get a good look at her face because she was wearing a white mask and had the blackest eyes he had ever seen in his life."

Keres.

These Velesan was not your typical Velesan. Their origins were unknown, only that they had been sent as children to be raised as Zeus's protectors. Around the same time, he had also sent Theo's enemy to train them and others. Afraid of the power that Nyx was amassing in such a short span of time, it was punishment and fear, one that Nyx had never forgotten.

Zeus had tried to weaken them.

It had only made them stronger.

When the Rrder was torn down, and Theo had been responsible for the destruction of it, Nyx had wowed retribution. They wore the white masks to shield their faces as a mark of who they were and it was clearly an indication that the twins who had made Theo's life as a child even more difficult, were in Ireland.

That was never a good thing.

"Theo."

Theo lifted her gaze to the Velesan who had raised her, who had been her father in all but blood, even if it was a fucked-up father-daughter relationship. Valerian had pushed her to almost breaking point on several occasions, under the premise that he was only making her stronger.

There had been little affection. No, that was something that Kaan had offered her.

Memories were sometimes like flood water. They rushed in and swept you away before you had a chance to tread the water.

Keres sank her nails into the flesh of Theo's scalp, causing her to yelp as the much stronger Velesan yanked her hair and tossed her against the cave wall. Theo had no chance to brace for impact before she crashed back first into the hard rock, the air leaving her lungs, a crack sounding and pain shooting through her skull.

Theo hit the ground a second later, her mouth slamming so hard her jaw rattled and she tasted her own blood. Theo tried to push herself up with her arms, but collapsed as tears pricked her eyes.

This was so unfair. Theo was years younger than Keres and she hadn't been training as long as Keres and her twin sister Eris had been. But time and time again, Valerian and Nyx made it so that Theo had her ass handed to her by one of the twins.

It was like they were trying to kill her.

That made her chest ache. Valerian was her guardian. He had taken her in and raised her when she was a child, and she knew nothing else. Once, when Theo and Kaan had sneaked out, they

*had gone to a little village in Romania and seen families. Fathers
who ruffled their son's hair, and mothers who held their daughter's
hands as they ate candied treats.*

*Kaan had taken her hand and told her that they were family
and would protect one another.*

But Kaan couldn't protect her from this onslaught.

Tomorrow would be the same. As would the day after that.

*Wake up. Fight for survival. Lose consciousness. Feed. Have
Kaan tend to her wounds if his weren't as bad as hers. Eat. Sleep.
Rinse. Repeat.*

*"Theo." Valerian's voice cut through her thoughts. Theo lifted
her head, ignoring the pain that seemed to echo throughout her
body.*

*"Theo," Valerian growled in a chastising way. "Get up off the
ground. Spit your blood out and bare your fangs. Go down savage.
Go down fighting."*

"Theo." Valerian's voice tore through her memories as he
sighed and got to his feet, buttoning up his jacket. "If Keres and
Eris are in Cork, then Nyx is not too far behind them. They may
not be responsible for the murders, but just because they did not
commit the crime does not mean that his hand did not guide the
blade. I will make some enquiries. Maisie, I could use your
ability."

It was not a direct order, and Theo noted that Maisie tensed,
then looked at Theo for a moment before she sighed and headed
out with Valerian, who held the door open for her as she ducked
under his arm.

Silas rose off his feet, holding Emery who was still asleep. He
blinked rapidly, as if that might put a halt to the pain he was no
doubt experiencing. "I'll go check on Blair. Are we opening today
or staying shut?"

Theo glanced at Kaan. "I think taking another night off is a
good idea. We won't have many revellers if the Gardaí are still
lurking about. But if anyone is in dire need of food, then we can
arrange a call out. Can you coordinate that?"

Silas nodded. "Ya, I can. I'll send Simon up so you can feed.

No arguments, Suzerain. We cannot have the leader of our Scion weakened while someone tried to attack our house."

He strode out then, leaving just Theo, Kaan, Kannon, and Carmen still on the phone. Theo shared a few more words with her Zayan and then she hung up, promising to contact Kaan with any more news.

"How long do you think it will take before the creepy twins make an appearance?" Kannon asked as he pushed off the counter and sheathed his knifes.

"Only when they want to." Kaan said with a exasperate sigh. "They will arrive in a flurry of violence and fear, drenched in blood, and hungry for destruction."

Kannon barked out a laugh. "You should write Christmas cards, you know. That was almost poetic if it wasn't disturbing as fuck."

That made Theo smile, despite the impending sense of foreboding that weighed down on her chest. Kannon had only encountered the twins on a few occasions, did not know the full extent of their cruelty. Theo liked to imagine that she had some sense of humanity in her veins. Keres and Eris had no such thing.

"Since we are staying shut today, I'm gonna go feed so Silas doesn't have an aneurysm." Theo glanced from Kaan to Kannon. "Then I'm gonna go for a walk, clear my head. Can I leave you two alone or do I need to call for a babysitter?"

Kaan tossed her a dark look, but Kannon just grinned. "I'll promise to try and behave."

Well, that wasn't really reassuring now, was it?

Theo shifted her gaze to Kaan, who was still lounging in his chair, looking very much the sultan as he ran a hand through his dark locks. "It will be grand, Theo. Stay alert. And check in so that Silas does not worry."

"You won't be worried about me?" Theo asked with a grin.

"Please. You are not the same girl they used to torment. You can almost kick my ass. I know that you would fight to the death to come home to us."

Theo was still grinning as she went up to her office, saw that Simon was already waiting for her. He lifted his gaze as she came in. Simon ran the human side of the security for Silas and he had been working for them for a long time. Tall and broad with reddish brown hair and a smattering of freckles across his cheeks and nose, Theo liked feeding from Simon because he never tried for more than just the high that came from being fed from. He knew sex wasn't part of the deal.

"Silas sent me up."

There was an apprehension in his voice, one that was laced with excitement. He stayed where he was sat on the couch in her office, and unbuttoned his shirt, exposing the pulse at his neck. Theo's gums throbbed as she walked over and reached to wrap a hand around Simon's throat.

The pulse quickened, and Theo took a deep breath as her fangs elongated. Still standing, Theo straddled Simon's thigh, then lowered her mouth to his throat, giving the column of his throat a long languid lick that made Simon shudder and made Theo close her eyes.

She shouldn't have done so.

When she closed her eyes, she imagined that it was Detective Sergeant De Barra's thigh she was straddling, that it was his pulse that was now galloping at the first graze of her teeth. She closed her mouth over the racing pulse, her hand still wrapped around Simon's throat to hold him in place as she felt a surge of hunger.

Sinking her fangs into the hot flesh, the first splash of blood spilled onto her tongue and Theo groaned, clenching her thighs around the thigh she was straddling. She swallowed down the blood, her eyes still closed, feeling unsatisfied in a way that she had not in a long time.

Theo drank her fill, almost glutting herself but it didn't stop her from wondering what the blood of a son of Cathain would taste like.

 **MAX**

Max had waited until Rían had fallen asleep on the couch before he attempted to make his escape. The idiot had been trying to nurse him since they had gotten back to his house. He'd lain there pretending to be asleep when Shauna had come home to grab a change of clothes and Rían and Shauna had a heated discussion.

"Well, he looks alive. That's a disappointment." Shauna said, sarcasm in her tone.

"You think you could stop being a brat for five minutes and ask if your brother is okay? Like, do you not want to know what happened him?"

"I would hazard a guess," Shaun replied in response to Rían's angry tone. "That Max pissed someone off. He has that kind of face. How many times have you said you wanted to brain his stubborn ass?"

Rían hissed through his teeth, *"That's beside the point. You treat him like shit, and he takes it because having you angry at him means you still feel something toward him. You could cut him some slack, Shauna. You can't keep blaming him for what your mam did."*

Max heard Rían grunt, knew that Shauna must have punched him or pushed him or something. *"You don't get to lecture me about my family, Rían. The moment I get access to my full trust fund, I'm out of here and then me and Max don't need to cross paths anymore. He can go back to his lonely fucking life with his dog and his work and you. I don't need him to act like my father. My father is nothing but maggots and dirt in the ground."*

Max had opened his eyes when Shauna had stormed out of

the house ten minutes later, slamming the door behind her. Rían had been standing by the window, his arms folded across his chest as he watched Shauna leave.

"I don't know why you try to get her to hate me a little less." Max had said, scrubbing a hand down his face, wincing at the sting of the scratches there.

"Because she's your family, Max. And without her and me, you'd be content to just work and hang with JD. It would make you a little less human."

Max had rolled his eyes, then gotten up to take some painkillers, forcing himself to eat the food Rían shoved in front of him. He'd tried to get his friend to go home, assuring him that he would be fine, but Rían had been adamant that he was staying where he was.

After checking in with Mike about the murder at the apartment, his boss had told him he didn't want to see his ass anywhere near the station for another twenty-four hours. Max had tried to argue, but Mike had told him that if he pushed the issue, he'd make Max take the holiday leave that had been built up.

So, Max had agreed, and turned his attention to getting Rían to leave. When it was clear there would be no shifting Rían, Max had feigned tiredness, reclining on the couch with JD's head in his lap. Max knew that he wouldn't or couldn't sleep because he had too much shite going on in his head.

After an hour of listening to some reality show that Rían had been watching, he heard the familiar almost purr of Rían's snoring that reminded him of the years they spent as roommates in boarding school. When the purr deepened, Max knew that the other man would be dead to the world now for at least six hours.

Max eased JD off his lap, giving the German Shepherd a scratch behind the ear before he grabbed his jacket and his car keys and headed out the front door. Night had slowly crept in, bringing darkness to settle over the skies. There was a kick to the wind, the kind that whipped into your face and as cut up as his face was, it stung with every lash.

But to feel pain is enough to prove you are alive.

His mam had said that to him when he had dislocated his shoulder playing rugby. It was something that stuck with him, even on days when he felt like he was numb to everything.

Max jumped into his Range Rover and headed out of the drive. Rían would have a fucking aneurysm when he woke up and Max was gone. The thought almost made Max smile.

He drove around the city, taking in the sights and sounds of the nighttime revellers. He was surprised to see that The Player's Lounge was shut again, and wondered how all this fucked up shit was tied to the petite owner of the club.

Max drove to one of the twenty four hour coffee places that he liked to go to when he was working a case and parked his car. Getting out of the car, he shoved his hands into his pockets and ignored the vibration of the phone.

Maybe he'd been wrong about Rían staying asleep for six hours.

Max was smiling as he walked into the little café, waving at the owner as he headed for the table he liked to frequent when he was holed up here. He took a seat, scanning his eyes at the exits and the patrons in the café.

There was Sally, the homeless woman who came in to get out of the cold. The owner of the café was good to those who needed a warm place to spend the night, and usually tried to give them jobs for some money. There was a couple who looked to be on their maybe third or fourth date, judging by the body language and the tentative looks.

He spotted the student in the corner with her books spread all the way across the booth that she was taking up, a pot of coffee and a half-eaten dinner. Max had asked her once what she was studying, had been pleasantly surprised to see that it was for a criminology degree. It had surprised her when Max introduced himself, then handed her his card in case she needed any direct quotes or sourcing for her assignments.

She glanced over and gave him a little wave, her gaze narrowing when she looked at his face, then she went back to her work when he inclined his head. The owner of the café, Paddy, came out from behind the counter himself and set down a steak and chips, and a large coffee.

"You looked like you needed that tonight, Lad. I've Irished up the coffee for ya."

Max chuckled as he thanked the man, then took a slug of the coffee and it made him cough. "Jesus Christ, Paddy. Did ya put any coffee in that at all?"

Paddy just laughed, his rounded belly vibrating as he replied. "Course I did, Max. You know I've no licence to serve the hard stuff. Couldn't have my favourite Detective having to arrest me."

He left Max to his meal then, and he cut into his steak, suddenly ravenous. This was the closest Max had felt to crashing in a long time. His body ached. It felt like he was hungry just because he had burned so much energy over the last couple of hours. It reminded him of the protein he had eaten coming up to a big rugby game.

But this felt like he hadn't eaten in days, and yet he'd eaten some of the food Rían had ordered only a few hours ago.

Max stabbed at another piece of steak with his fork and shovelled it into his mouth. Paddy made the nicest steak in Cork City and it made him think of the time he had taken Vanessa here, and how she'd nearly gotten sick at the sight of his rare steak.

Then again, Vanessa had taken out a wipe to clean the table because she thought the place was dirty. Max had told her to stop being so stuck up and continued to eat his steak as she poked at her salad.

His gut twisted a second before he heard a voice speak.

"Detective Sergeant."

Max blinked and Theodora Caden was standing by his booth. She seemed shorter than Max had initially thought, but no less striking. He ran his eyes over her in a quick assessment. She was wearing black pants that came down past her knees, a corset that was trimmed with gold stitching and cogs of some sort. Over the corset, covering her breasts, she had a cropped black jacket with more gold stitching and design. The jacket was fasted at her throat.

On her feet, she wore black flat trainers, and, on her head, she wore an old bowler hat with goggles on it. She looked like a character from a steampunk novel.

She arched a brow when Max had been assessing her for too long. Theo Caden leaned on the seat and inclined her head. "You've been in the wars since we last spoke."

Her voice sounded like whiskey and honey, husky and smooth. Her lips curved into a smile and Max leaned back in his seat before he answered her.

"Nothing as dramatic. Rescued a cat up a tree for an old lady. Cat wasn't too happy."

Theo barked out a surprise laugh that seemed to startle even herself. "I know a thing or two about asshole cats, but I did not know Garda had a sense of humour."

Max knew that he wasn't the best at flirting, didn't have time for it, but he needed to charm Theo in case she knew more than she was letting on about all the murders. He'd spent enough time around Rían...it shouldn't be that hard.

"I'm off the clock, Ms. Caden. The sense of humour is allowed on a night off."

The smile that Theo gave him was dazzling, but Max had the distinct feeling that Theo was sizing him up as much as he was assessing her. She glanced around, then pointed to the seat opposite Max. "May I?"

Max nodded, making a show of cutting another piece of his steak and eating it as Theo slid into the seat across from him. He felt the weight of her gaze on him as he chewed his meat, then popped a chip into his mouth before washing it down with his coffee infused whiskey.

"Ms. Caden-" He started only for Theo to cut across him.

"Theo, please... since you're off the clock and all that Jazz, Detective Sergeant."

Max smiled, or well, he tried to smile without looking like a serial killer as Rían often said of his inability to look normal with a smile on his face.

"Then, it's Max."

There was a little twinkle in her eyes as she opened her mouth to speak, pausing when Paddy came over with a take-away cup and a wrapped sandwich, setting them down in front of Theo. She grinned at the man, then slid a fifty euro toward him.

"Cheers, Paddy. Make sure Sally's got a full belly before she heads out in the morning. I tried to convince her that I'd somewhere for her to stay but she told me she was grand. I left a new waterproof sleeping bag at the counter too. She'll take it from you faster than me."

Paddy gave Theo's shoulder a squeeze, then glanced between Max and Theo with a massive smile.

"He thinks we're on a date." Theo said obviously amused, then the grin deepened when Max snorted, and it dimpled her cheeks.

"Paddy knows me well enough to know I don't date."

Max paused midbite, unsure why he had just said that to the woman he suspected might be a murderer. His stomach was all twisted, but he kept eating. Theo lifted her coffee to her lips, then glanced at his plate.

As he was still trying to appear all charming and shit, Max offered her his plate, very shocked as Theo snagged a chip from his plate, dipped it in the blood from his steak and popped it into her mouth. The little moan that tumbled from her lips had Max's body hard in seconds.

"Damn, that's good. Makes my sandwich seem like a boring ass salad now."

Max chuckled. "Not a fan of salad, I take it?"

This time, it was Theo who snorted. "Fuck no. It's alright in small doses, but I like a decent meal. I suppose that's a turn off for men who think women should be slim and watch what they eat."

Max shook his head, as Theo stole another chip and he watched as she repeated the same action as before, dipping it into the blood before she threw it into her mouth. "I don't think there's anything wrong with enjoying the food you eat. Life is very fucking short. Eat what the fuck you want. It hasn't done you any harm, has it."

Theo regarded him with amusement. "Why, Max, if I was any

other woman and not one of your suspects in some murders, I would think you were flirting with me."

"That has nothing to do with it." Max said, taking another bite of his steak before carrying on. "I can't flirt. My best friend tells me I was born without the ability to be charming."

Theo offered him a warm smile that had Max wondering who was playing who at the table. "I don't think you give yourself enough credit, Max. If this really was a date, then maybe you'd have gotten to first base."

Max said nothing as he finished his meal, drinking the coffee slowly to wash down the food. Theo stayed where she was, trying to give off the appearance that she was just passing the time away.

"Did you drive here, Theo? If not I could drive you somewhere."

Theo arched her brows at him. "Is that your line to try and get into my knickers?"

Max almost choked on his coffee and that had Theo laughing.

"No... I mean..." Max stuttered and realized that Rían had been right. He was fucking awful at this shite.

Clearing his throat, Max tried again. "What I meant to say was that if there is someone out there targeting you, then it might not be safe to be walking the streets by yourself."

"Ah," Theo said as she picked up her travel cup and her sandwich. "So, you were aiming for chivalrous and not sleazy."

He ignored the twisting in his stomach and ran a hand through his hair. "I told ya I wasn't any good at being charming and flirting."

"So, you were flirting with me."

Max tried for an easy smile. "Guilty as charged, Garda. Do you need to borrow my handcuffs?"

Theo grinned, her haunting green eyes slowly caressing his body before they came back up to hold his gaze. "Kinky, Detective Sergeant. I'm impressed."

Max felt a thrill course through him. How had this fact-finding mission turned into a flirty conversation that had Max wanting to take the woman home to his bed. Or hell, even to the fucking back seat of his SUV. There shouldn't be this sort of attraction with someone who was intrinsically linked to the deaths of multiple people.

"I'd better head back."

"Let me walk ya out." Max said as he stood and threw some money on the table.

"Stay and finish up. I'm a big girl, Max."

Max shook his head, motioning for Theo to head out. "I was leaving anyways."

Theo tilted her head, her green eyes like gemstones as she said. "Are you asking me to walk out first so you can check out my ass."

Max felt his cheeks heat, which made Theo laugh again, a lyrical sort of sound.

"Just being chivalrous, Ms. Caden."

Theo pressed her lips together in a slight pout before she started to walk out, the sway of her hips no doubt to prove a point as she glanced over her shoulder with a feisty grin. "Whatever you say, Detective Sergeant."

Max rolled his eyes as she followed her out, lifting his hand in a goodbye to Paddy. Theo stood for a moment in the carpark, her face tilted toward the moon, and she looked even more relaxed, like she felt as much comfort in the dark as he did.

"Are ya sure you don't want a lift?" Max asked as she turned to look at him.

"Nah, I'm grand. But thanks. For a Garda, you're not too bad."

Max let loose a chortle of laughter. "For a murder suspect, you're not too bad either."

Theo was shaking her head as she turned away and headed across the car park. The unease in his stomach started to dissipate, but awareness prickled his senses. He was already striding toward Theo when he heard the screech of tyres.

Max wasn't sure how he moved so quickly. One minute he was watching the car hurtling toward Theo as she walked across the carpark. Then next he felt the kiss of the car against his hip as he all but rugby tackled Theo to the ground. He covered her smaller frame with his, lifting his head to try and get a glance at the licence plate before the car vanished but the car had no plates, and all Max could make out in the dark was that it was a run of the mill sedan.

Max yanked his phone out of his pocket and placed a call. "Ya this is Detective Sergeant Max De Barra, badge number CK666. I'm in the car park of Paddy's café and someone just tried to run over a Ms. Theodora Caden. Call Mike O'Connor and tell him what happened. It's in relation to The Player's Lounge killings."

Max hung up and looked at Theo. She'd lost her hat in the scuffle, her orange hair splayed out on the ground. She had a weird expression on her face, which had Max narrowing his gaze.

"You okay?"

"You're badge number is 666?" Then she giggled, a very feminine sound that had Max thinking that Theodora Caden was a hell of a lot more than he had been expecting.

She'd almost been mowed down by a car and she was laying there laughing at his badge number. What the fuck?

THEO

Theo had heard the screech of tyres a second after she sensed the danger and had already been angling her body to brace for attack when Max tackled her to the ground. She would have deftly avoided getting struck on her own merit, but that might alert the Detective Sergeant that Theo was not all that human.

He wouldn't have been screaming "There be a vampire!", though it definitely would have made him even more suspicious.

Theo had seen how fast Max had moved, tearing across the carpark like he himself was a vampire. The man might not know that the blood of Cathain flowed through his veins, however the powers that being a descendant of the legendary Irish vampire hunter were definitely coming to the surface.

Made Theo wonder if the sister had also started to display the same hunter traits.

Max was looking at her with this strange expression, like he was trying to fit together the pieces of the puzzle that was Theo and just couldn't. She had laughed when she found out that his badge number was 666, and almost made a joke about him being Detective Dracula.

Theo was acutely aware that Max had the hard line of his body pressed against hers. They were just there, on the ground, holding each other's gaze and Theo was struck by an urge to brush the dark strands of his hair from his eyes.

Max tilted his head and Theo blinked, the pulse at his neck beating in rhythm with his heartbeat. She could roll them so that she was pinning him down, sink her fangs into his throat and drink from him. Max might be able to stop her, but Theo felt like she was willing to risk it.

Then she had an image in her head of Max sliding his cock into her right before she sank her fangs into his flesh.

Fucking hell, Kaan was right. Theo really needed to get laid.

Shoving down all the dirty thoughts in her head, Theo placed her hands on Max's chest. "You gonna let me up, Detective Sergeant?"

That seemed to drag Max out of whatever thought process was going on in his head, because he got up with a fluid grace that most humans didn't have, then held out his hand to help Theo up. She got to her feet, then glanced around for her hat. She spotted it to the side by the wheel of a car, went over and lifted it up and turned it over in her hands before returning it to her head.

Max was scanning the area, as if he was looking for clues as to who might have tried to run her over. He glanced over at Theo, his dark brows almost touching as he studied her.

"Do you still think that the murders are unrelated to you and your club?" Max asked, his tone tight as Theo fished her phone out of her pocket, happy that it hadn't been damaged in the fall.

She began to shoot off a text to Kaan as she answered Max's question with an amused tone. "Maybe the driver just had a shit car that had no brakes and needed to have his headlights replaced. I mean, he probably saw you and since your whole vibe screams Garda, and he panicked. Perhaps he was trying to get away from you so fast that he just didn't see me."

Max rolled his eyes. "I'm not sure anyone could miss you with that hair colour."

Theo put a hand to her chest as if to feign surprise. "Did you just make a joke? Letting that sense of humour come out to play again, Detective Sergeant?"

Max grunted, muttering under his breath that he was getting a headache when the sound of sirens came roaring down the road. A black unmarked car sped into the carpark and ground to halt just shy of where they stood. The passenger door opened and a man in his forties got out, his eyes trained on Max.

"What part of my order to stay home was not clear to you lad?"

Theo could hear the worry in the man's tone, like he was angry and afraid at the same time because it was what she some-times sounded like when chewing out any of the members of her Scion. Being the head bitch in charge wasn't all power and titles... you worried...a lot.

"You told me not to work the case, and I didn't. I came out for some food. Then I bumped into Ms. Caden and as I walked out to my car, someone tried to take her out with a car. I believe some would call that a coincidence, sir."

Theo wanted to laugh at the sincerity in Max's tone, and this boss of Max's arched a greying brow at him and shook his head. "What the hell do I expect from you? It's not like you listen to me at all."

The corner of Max's lips twitched, like he was trying to hold back a laugh and Theo took a step closer to the two men, glancing at Max. "That must have been some cat you rescued if your boss is worried about you."

The older Garda looked from Theo to Max as Max just shrugged. "All part of the job. Sir, this is Ms. Theo Caden. She owns The Player's Lounge."

The Garda held out his hand. "Ms. Caden, Superintendent Mike O'Connor. Are you hurt? Do you need medical attention?"

Theo shook her head. "Nah, I'm grand. Detective Sergeant De Barra here saved me from any real injury."

This Superintendent Mike O'Connor assessed Theo and then asked her if she had thought about anyone who might want to cause her harm. Theo twirled a strand of hair between her fingers and gave a little shrug.

"As I told Max here, I'm sure it was all a misunderstanding and has nothing to do with the murders. I wish I had more infor-mation for you, Superintendent, but that's all I got."

Mike's lips parted as if he had more questions when a sleek black Audi TT drove into the carpark, purring as it did. Theo suppressed a grin as the engine cut off, and the door opened.

Kaan swung his legs out of the sports car, stretched to his full height, then buttoned up his jacket.

A crowd had gathered to try and see what had happened, and why the police were gathering in the café's carpark, and both women and men turned to watch as Kaan all but glided across the carpark toward them. He ignored to Gardaí, focused on Theo as he ran his eyes over her.

"Are you hurt?"

Theo rolled her eyes. "I'm fine." She glanced at the Gardaí watching the interaction. "Kaan, you already know Detective Sergeant De Barra. But this is Superintendent Mike O'Connor. Superintendent this is Kaan Sydin, my business partner and family."

Theo watched as Max and Kaan exchanged a frosty look, and Theo elbowed Kaan in the ribs, earning a glare from the other Velesan. Theo lifted her brows as if to tell him to behave, but Kaan just grinned, extended his hand.

"Pleasure to meet you, Superintendent."

He was using his best behaviour tone, and Theo almost barked out a laugh as Max threw him a look that called bullshit on Kaan's statement. Max folded his arms across his chest and Theo could scent the alpha vibes coming off him.

It should have annoyed her...she hated men thinking that they owned her...but it had her wondering if Max was feeling possessive because she was a murder suspect, or if he was feeling the attraction too?

It was insane...utterly insane, right? They were supposed to be mortal enemies.

She'd seen Buffy...she knew how that all went tits up...

"We would just like to document your statement, Ms. Caden."

Theo shifted her gaze to look at Max. "I'm sure you can recount the events better than me, Detective Sergeant. I only knew what was happening when I heard the tyres and you rugby tackled me to the ground. That's my statement. If you need anything else, you know where I work and where I live."

Max's lips pressed together in a firm line, and when he went to say more, his boss stopped him.

"That's all for tonight, Ms. Caden. Stay vigilant and let us know if anything else like this happens. Your safety is paramount."

Theo inclined her head, felt Kaan's hand land on the small of her back as he steered her towards his Audi, opening the passenger door for her. Max had yet to take his eyes off her, and even with the door closed, it felt like he was still staring at her.

Kaan got in beside her and started the engine, not saying anything until they were driving away from the scene of the crime. "I told you to stay alert. Not go on a date with the man who has a bug up his ass about you and the club."

There was a growl in his tone, a chastising that irked Theo. "I was alert. I went to get a sandwich and a coffee, both of which I don't have now and I'm starving. Max was already there when I arrived, and I tried to gauge his reaction. That was it until the fucking car tried to run me over. Don't get pissy at me because I called you to collect me."

Kaan blew out a long breath. "I'm not pissy because you wanted me to play taxi, Theo. I'm pissed because you have little regard for your own safety and forget that if something happens to you, then the Scion is broken."

"You'd hold it together, Kaan."

"No." He replied in a harsh and certain tone. "I would be the most broken. We have been family since that very first moment, Theo, and I could not bear to lose you. It would unravel me. Unravel all of us."

Theo didn't respond to that, just reached over and gave Kaan's knee a squeeze. She told Kaan to bring her to The Player's Lounge so that she could change her clothes so as not to worry the rest of the Scion. She took off her hat, frowned when she saw the crack in her goggles.

"Dammit, I liked those googles." She said with a resigned sigh.

"I'm sure we can find you more googles. You need a new pair of pants too, darling, if those marks don't come out in the wash."

Kaan pulled up outside The Player's Lounge but left the engine running. "Want me to hang on for you?"

Theo unbuckled her seat belt. "You not got anywhere else to be? Or are you just trying to babysit me?"

Kaan grinned, giving a nonchalant shrug of his shoulders. "A little bit of both. Since everyone is off tonight, the Scion is having a little gathering at the house. I find that I am a little too morose for partying tonight."

Kaan got like this sometimes. Hell, Theo got like it sometimes. It was one of the curses of immortality, of having lived so long that the things that were once their lifeblood, the things that excited them no longer did. Theo had felt like that prior to all the murders. Kaan was feeling the loneliness of being old as dirt and Theo knew that she would be there for him, as he had always been there for her.

"Why don't you park the car, and follow me in? We can bask in the quiet before we eventually must head home."

Theo got out of the car when Kaan nodded, then headed into the empty building. Theo loved coming in here when no one else was in. It seemed eerily peaceful. No music, no cheering, no patrons falling down drunk and no scents or sounds of sex and blood.

She called for the elevator, pressing the button to go all the way up to her office where she had a few changes of clothes for certain occasions. The elevator opened and Theo instantly became alert. The closer she got to her office, the surer she was that she wasn't alone on the floor.

She pulled out her phone and sent a text to Kaan to tell him to stay away. He probably wouldn't listen to her, but she had to try and keep him safe.

Shoving her phone back into her pocket, Theo twisted the handle of the door to her office and thrust it open. Darkness surrounded her as she stepped inside and trained her eyes on the figure in the shadows.

Taking a step into the room, Theo placed her hands on her hips, then assessed the intruder. Tall and lean with black hair that was pulled back into a ponytail, his face was a thing of beauty, like it had been carved from marble in the ancient temples of Greece. Piercing blue eyes that seemed at odds with the harsh beauty of his face held hers as Theo flicked on the light in the office.

Nyx, God of night, was sat in Theo's office chair, a glass of what looked like blood at his lips as he drank then set the beverage down on the table. Theo lifted her gaze to the sword encased in glass above his head, her father's sword, and her finger's itched to go to it, take it in her grasp and behead the asshole smirking at her.

"Nyx, had I known you were coming, I'd have thrown you a party. Really, you should have called."

The smirk on Nyx's face grew and when he spoke, Theo heard the power in his tone.

"You know I like to surprise you, my love. I heard that you were in a spot of bother, so had to come see for myself."

"You'd think you'd be more in the know, considering it's your hand that guides these murders." Theo accused Nyx, watching to see if he gave away any slip with his expression, but all he did was laugh, and the sound felt like pinpricks on her skin.

"It is not my hand that guides this murderer, love. I am merely an interested party. Eris and Keres are enjoying the hunt."

Nyx got to his feet with a fluidity that spoke of the many centuries as trainer in the Order of the Dragon, and his status as a Greek god. His power was so great that Zeus sent him away from Mount Olympus in fear that Nyx might just rebel against him and win. Theo had seen his powers over the years and been victim to them a time or two.

Nyx had the ability to remove the senses of any human or vampire, even the Velesan. He could take one sense at a time, make you blind, then steal your hearing. He liked to torture his victims in this manner, prolonging the sense of confusion and fear. And then he would let you have it all back for a split second before taking all your senses from you at once.

He was also the reason why Theo had but one Zayan left that she had sired.

When Theo was younger, only a teenager in Velesan years, Theo had noted how Nyx had become fixated on her. It started when she began to master her power of astral projection. The first time Theo had beaten Keres in a fight. When her body changed and she became a woman in Nyx's eyes, he started to crave more.

It started with a tuck of her hair, then brown, behind her ears. A familiar touch. A longing look. Trying to separate her from Kaan. From Valerian. Then the gifts started, innocent at first and then bordering on inappropriate.

Valerian must have said something to Nyx because although his actions didn't stop, they didn't go any further. When Theo was seventeen, Nyx made his intentions clear. He had wanted her. She would become his mate, and she would bear him powerful Velesan.

Theo had rejected him, telling him that she would never willingly be his.

She had thought the matter over, but when her and Kaan had started to dismantle the Order of the Dragon, and begun to create Zayan of their own, Nyx butchered them all, telling Theo that without him, she would always feel the loss of her children.

Nyx strode around the desk, walking toward Theo as she jerked her head up in defiance. Nyx reached a hand out, wrapped his fingers around her throat. Theo stayed still, willing her heartrate to not betray her as Nyx used his other hand to pop the button on her jacket, then moved the hand at her throat down to the swell of her breast.

"Like the finest wine, you become more alluring with age. If I licked your skin, I bet I could taste the power in your blood."

She heard the elevator whir to life, as Nyx grinned, and blood stained his teeth. "I'm not behind all of this, love. If I wanted you dead, then you would know it was me. I'd fuck you before I killed you. I've fantasised about the warmth of your flesh as I sink into you. I'll see you soon, my love."

Nyx let go of her so fast that she stumbled forward, spinning round as the elevator doors opened and Kaan strode out, a sword in his hand but Nyx had already vanished. Theo went to her desk, got out some wipes and scrubbed the parts of her skin that Nyx had touched.

"You good?" Kaan asked her.

"No. But Nyx isn't behind the murders. His exact words were that he would want to fuck me before he killed me."

Kaan frowned, setting his sword on the bookshelf by the door. "Then who the fuck is behind all this and what does it mean that it brought Nyx and the twin bitches to Cork?"

Theo had no clue, but worry gnawed at her as she considered who might be the one killing all her staff if not Nyx? And now that Nyx was back, how the fuck would she finally figure out how to kill him and rid the world of him?

But to kill Nyx, you had to kill his guard dogs and it was not such an easy thing to kill fear and pain... Theo knew that all too well.

MAX

Max had stood there and listened as Mike chewed him out, then did as he was told, and went home to get a second earful from Rían when he found out what had happened. Then he'd made Max sit down so he could give him the once over, flipping Max off when Max pointed out that he wasn't a real doctor and most of his patients were dead.

"Still went to medical school, asshole. Though I can't fix stupid."

Once Rían had been certain that Max was not going to die, and obviously could be left to his own devices now, he left telling Max he'd check in with him later. Max had rooted out his files and started to reread the information he had already committed to memory, hoping something else jumped out to him.

He'd then gone for a run, then showered and went to the station before the sun had risen. Mike hadn't been happy that he had showed up, but it was all hands-on deck, and they were no closer to pinpointing a suspect. Max was almost positive that Theo wasn't the murderer, even if he knew that she was hiding something.

Then the trail went cold.

After two weeks of bodies showing up, there was suddenly a lapse. Max wondered if the killer had simply glutted himself on killing and was taking time to let the urge build once again. Max knew that the reprieve would be short lived, and that when the killer re-emerged from whatever pit he was in, the bloodshed would be far more than they had seen.

Like a junkie who needed its next fix...the killer had a taste of blood and he wanted more.

After three shifts of waiting for the next body to drop, Mike sent them all home to take a day to rest. Max had wanted to stay but knew Mike would just push until Max agreed. He knew Max too well because he told Max to stay away from the investigation, and more specifically to stay away from Theo Caden.

Max had come home late, checking on Shauna to see she was asleep, her friend Megan beside her in the bed, before he went to bed himself. After a few hours of tossing and turning and a nightmare, Max got up, showered, and threw on a pair of jeans and a t-shirt. The smell of a fry greeted him as he came downstairs and headed into the kitchen.

Shauna looked over at him in a mixture of surprise and annoyance as Megan smiled in greeting.

"I thought you were at work."

"I was," Max said as he went to the fridge and took out an energy drink. "Got home late."

"Well, I only put on enough food for two."

Max leaned over and grabbed a slice of toast. "I'm good."

Shauna frowned but Max turned, and Megan let out a gasp. She was looking at the scratches on his face that was almost healed but still looked horrible. The other woman looked at him with the same look women got when they wanted to be the one to heal you. Like Max was broken and she could change him.

He'd seen it enough times in Vanessa's eyes.

"Shauna said a murderer attacked you. That you could have died." Megan said dreamily.

For fuck sake, all he needed now was an oversized tween looking at him like he was a hero.

"It's grand. I'm sure Shauna wasn't worried too much."

Shauna laughed, turning the sausages over in the pan. "I wasn't worried at all. Rían was. If you died then it means I get my money sooner than you'll give it to me so I call that a win."

Megan sucked in a breath in shock, but Max just chuckled and tugged at the ends of Shauna's braid. "I love you too. I'm heading out for the day so you'll have the house to yourselves until later."

Shauna stopped what she was doing, and glared at Max. "You're going to see her."

It was a statement rather than a question, as Max grabbed another slice of toast from the pile on the counter. "Ya, I am. You could come with me if you want."

"Hard pass. I never want to see that bitch again."

Max didn't want to be having this argument in front of someone who wasn't family, but Shauna was clearly in the mood to fight. It was the same old argument every time that Max went to see their mother, and then even if Shauna might have thawed toward him, she froze him out again.

"She's still your mam, Shauna. She's unwell."

"Do you think that of all the killers you hunt down? Did you think that Erasmus Finn was unwell when you killed him?" Shauna hissed at him, and Max felt his temper flare, knew he should dampen it but something dark in him wanted to lash out.

"Erasmus Finn was a monster who acted on his urges and kidnapped and raped children. He's lucky all I did was put a bullet in him and that I had a child to save. The world is a horrible place, Shauna, so maybe check your privilege before you talk shit about the woman who ensures you can do your poncy arts degree, and the brother who works to ensure you never have to worry about being a victim of circumstance."

Shauna looked like she was close to tears and there was this voice inside of Max that crooned at him to hurt her more. Adrenaline pumped inside his veins, and he was shocked at how good it felt as he grabbed his car keys and headed out the door, stopping to grab his leather jacket.

"You are just like her, yano. Cold. Indifferent. She took away the only parent who showed us affection and you are just like her. It's like you're not even human. Are you gonna snap and kill me like she killed dad one day?" Shauna shouted after him and Max slammed the front door so hard it rattled.

Getting in his jeep, he reversed so fast it kicked up the gravel on the drive. He turned the music up full blast, letting Sleep Token pound from the speakers. He was angry as fuck and needed to calm down before he visited his mother.

Aideen might be locked in her mind a lot of the time, but she always seemed to know when he was agitated or restless. He knew he shouldn't have said those things to Shauna, but she had hit a nerve. He was cold. He was distant. But he never recalled his mother being like that.

His mam had been strict with him, while his dad had been a little more lenient. She was the one who made him think of exercise as part of his routine, a stress release. She was the one who educated him on different cultures and mythology. Shauna had been younger, but his lessons had started when he was seven or eight, however his mam never put the effort into Shauna like she had him.

"Shauna's not like you and me. Her life will be different to yours. One day, you'll understand why."

Max had never understood, and it was unlikely that he ever would.

He drove out of the city, headed down the M8, passed by Glanmire, Fermoy and Mitchelstown before he drove in the direction of Mallow. Max had taken the long way round just to cool off on the drive over, and then suddenly the residential home was looming in front of him.

Max parked the SUV, then leaned his head back against the headrest as he debated just going home. Well, maybe not home, but somewhere else, somewhere not here. What was the point in coming here anymore to spend an hour or two in silence, or listening to Aideen rant, before leaving her here again.

Max closed his eyes, thinking back to the night his father had died. He recalled every moment of that night and yet, he felt like there was a part he was missing, a snippet of vital information that could piece together the horrible events so that they would make sense.

Max jogged down the stairs, glancing at his watch to see that he had a few minutes before Rian picked him up to go to the party. He hadn't wanted to go. His mam had been distracted today and she had yelled at Shauna twice already. Max had gone to his sister to comfort her, and he didn't want to leave her alone when their dad wasn't there to act as a buffer.

"I don't know where he is, Brendan. It's been two weeks since he went off to do the consult and there's been no contact. He wasn't himself when he went off." There was a pause and then his mam said. "Brendan, I'll call you back."

His mam called his name then in the weird way she always knew that he was there. She set the phone down as he came in, gave him a broad smile. "You look nice."

Max rolled his eyes. "I'd much prefer to just stay home."

Aideen laughed, then gave his shoulder a squeeze. "Enjoy these nights for as long as you can, Max. One day the weight of being an adult will be a burden you have to carry."

Rían had blared his horn then, and Aideen had ushered him toward the door.

"Is everything okay, mam?" Max had asked, standing in the open door.

His mam had smiled, though it looked fake as hell to Max. "It is. Go and have some fun, Max."

Max opened his eyes. He'd never been able to find out who this Brendan was or how his parents knew him. It was something that Max had always wondered. The Gardaí investigating the murder had told him that his mam hadn't been talking to anyone on the phone...that it had all been part of her delusion. They hadn't taken Max's statement too seriously, and even when Max had become a guard himself, he hadn't been able to find any evidence that this Brendan was a real person.

Getting out of the car, Max locked it, then strode toward the entrance. The care facility was supposed to be a home away from home for residents whose mental health issues kept them away from their real homes. Max had often felt like the cheeriness of the staff had to be a front because no one could be surrounded by this much sadness and sickness and be that happy.

The receptionist gave him a bright smile as she buzzed him in, and Max walked down the long hallway toward his mother's room. During her first few months here, Max had to have her reassigned to different rooms because she kept trying to escape. She's put a nurse and an orderly in hospital trying to get out the window. Now his mother had a lovely room with iron bars on the windows and a door that was always closed.

A woman was standing at the nurses' station, and she glanced down the hall the moment she heard footsteps. She gave him a genuine smile. Max had known the nurse since his mother was first admitted and had paid a fortune to ensure that the nurse stayed on as his mam's primary carer.

Adisa had been born in South Africa and had come to Ireland to be with her husband who was Irish. They'd married young, and Adisa had been in her mid-twenties when Max had first met her.

"Max," she said with a grin. "I've missed your handsome face."

Max chuckled, rolling his eyes. "Your husband know that you flirt with Gardaí?"

"He knows it keeps me out of parking tickets."

Adisa glanced toward the door of his mam's room. "She has been agitated the last few days. Suddenly calmed down. As if she knew today her son would visit."

"You believe too much in that hoodoo voodoo shit, Adisa."

She wiggled her finger at Max. "Mock me all you want, boy. But I have seen the dead rise in my village and terrorise the living."

Max was shaking his head as he opened the door to his mam's room and stepped inside, making sure it was locked behind him. Aideen De Barra was sat by the window, hugging her knees to her chest, a shawl around her shoulders. She looked thinner than she had been the last time Max had been to see her. She didn't spare him a glance as Max looked around the room, saw that not much had changed either.

"Hey mam, it's me, Max."

Eyes that once were filled with a keen intelligence now just looked half crazed as they slid to look at him. Aideen inhaled through her nose, her face contorting as she spoke to Max for the first time in months.

"You come to me smelling of Velesan. You reek of vampires."

Max reached up and pinched the bridge of his nose. So today

he was back to dealing with insane Aideen. Right. Fanfuckintastic. This was already a waste of time.

Aideen tilted her head ever so slightly. "You have felt it. That knot in your stomach. The loathing. They walk among you and you are blind to them. My fault. My fault. I left you untrained."

His mam looked at the healing marks on his face and she smiled, a feral kind of smile. "Maybe I trained you just enough. You survived one of them. But not the one you smell of. No. Another Velesan."

Aideen was just talking gibberish. Max didn't understand what she was saying. She had made up this world in her head and now she was telling Max about it. He'd never heard her mention the term Velesan before. He made not of it to research when he got home.

"Do you remember your lessons, Max?"

"Which lessons were those, mam?" Max answered her question with a question and that only made her grin a little more.

Aideen pulled the shawl around her even tighter. "Tell me what you know of the Abhartach."

"Which version would you like to hear, mam?"

Her brown eyes looked at him. "The version I taught you. The real version."

Max felt like he should humour her, considering this was the most conversation that he'd gotten from her that was constructed of full sentences. He leaned back in his seat, resting his palms on his thighs before he began to speak.

"When Ireland was a land of chieftains and druids, of Saints and scholars, there once roamed a creature who feed on the blood of humans and used their own blood to turn the dead into monsters. He was called the Abhartach. He was thought killed and was buried, but he rose once more from the grave and went in search of fresh blood to regain his strength."

Max paused but his mam motioned with her hand for him to continue.

"There was a chieftain named Cathain who wanted to free the country of the Abhartach. He goes to consult two men of faith, a Saint, and a druid. The Saint told Cathain that the only way to kill the Vampire was to find a sword made from yew wood. The Saint advised Cathain that, once the Abhartach was killed, he would need to bury him upside down and that he would need to find a great stone to lock it in for good.

But Cathain was an ordinary man. So, the druid he spoke to told him that the Abhartach could only be defeated by someone of rivalled strength, one not cursed with a lust for blood drinking. Through a pagan ritual and a blood sacrifice, the druid imbued Cathain with the power to defeat the Abhartach."

His mam smiled, like she was proud of him. "Good. Good. You didn't forget. No need for a sword made from a yew wood. Stab them through the heart, the brain. Cut off their heads and burn the bodies. You watch. You watch the body for days and watch as it withers to old age. It takes time but the truth is always there."

Max heaved out a breath. This was getting him nowhere. Max leaned forward in his seat then pushed off to stand up straight. "I'm gonna head out, mam. I'll see you soon."

He angled his body away and saw a blur of movement a moment before his mam grabbed his arms, her eyes wide. "Son of Cathain. That is who you are. My legacy passed to you. You have felt it, I can tell, in your veins, in your gut. You know who the Abhartach are. Look a little closer, Maximillian. Remember your lessons."

She let go of him abruptly, and went to sit back down, her eyes glazed once more as she looked out the window. Max walked to the door, his legs a little shaky as he twisted the handle to let himself out.

It was then he heard his mother whisper. "They think I don't know that there is a vampire working here. I can smell him. I can feel it. He will not have my blood."

Max didn't take a breath until he was out of the room and leaning against the door. He wasn't sure what had just happened, but he was leaving with more questions than answers. Adisa asked him if he was okay, and Max tried to assure her that he was alright.

He'd been with his mother for longer than he thought as the

early winter night had settled in while he was with her. Max said a quick goodbye to Adisa, then hurried along the corridor to get outside. His heart was pounding, and his mother's words kept ringing through in his head.

"Son of Cathain. That is who you are. My legacy passed to you."

Max clearly wasn't paying attention as he bumped into a male nurse who was just coming out of a resident's room. Max was about to offer an apology when his nose caught the scent of copper and his stomach clenched so hard that he thought he might pass out.

The man reached out toward him. "Steady there, bud. You're just gonna walk away now, aren't ya?"

There was a sharp pain in his gut. He'd felt that pain only once before in his life. When he'd first met Theodora Caden. What connected these two together?

As if on instinct, Max just continued walking and fought the urge to say something to the man. Maybe he was going mad. His last CT scan hadn't indicated any changes to his brain structure but that was six months ago. He night need a new one.

Max wasn't certain of anything much right now, but there was one thing he was absolutely clear on.

The twist in his gut had vanished the moment he was away from the nurse.

# THEO

Theo had not slept for the last couple of days. To be honest, she kept expecting Nyx to show up in her room. When she had arrived home with Zaan the night Nyx had paid her a visit, Emery had been sitting on the bottom step of the stairs, waiting for them.

"The Lord of Night is back."

Theo sucked in a gulp of air to try and tell Emery that she was safe, but she couldn't lie to the Zayan any more than she could lie to herself.

Kaan had just gone over and ruffled her hair, telling her that yes, Nyx had come by but he wouldn't dare come here.

Emery had looked at Theo. Hard.

Then she had gotten to her feet and stomped up the stairs without saying another word.

They had opened The Player's Lounge last night for a private party, basically inviting vampires in so they could feed and that in private and Theo could make sure that no vampire was hungry enough to drain a human to death.

They'd had a few days and nights off from the bodies hitting the floor and Theo was grateful. They'd made enough money last night to make up for the time the club was closed. And they were hosting their vampire night in a couple of days.

That was always a popular night.

No one batting an eyelid at the couple going at it in the darkened corner and assumed the blood on any exposed flesh was fake. The event was already sold out since Maisie had put the tickets up for sale online. It should be a good night for everyone involved.

Theo headed down the stairs to get something to eat before she headed out to The Player's Lounge. She heard a commotion in the main entertainment room, so she veered off in that direction to see Blair sitting down on the couch and a very pissed off Emery in the fireside chair.

She blinked when she looked at Emery. Her lips were painted a ruby red, and she wore too much makeup for her pale skin. Somehow, from someone's closet, she had stolen a red leather mini skirt and a matching bra. Her hair had been curled and she looked like a teenager playing dress up.

"Hey, what I miss?" Theo asked as she crossed the room and leaned against the fireplace.

From the clench in Blair's jaw, it wasn't good.

"I want to go to the vampire night."

"Okay..." said Theo, not sure what was so bad about that.

"And I want to have sex."

Theo glanced at Blair who just held out her hands. Emery had been raped during her time in the brothel, and while she was an adult, there were monsters out there who looked at her and saw a child and used that to justify their actions.

Nyx had used Emery.

There were times when Emery was able to function normally. There were times when they could take her to the club, and it would be fine. But throwing her into a night that was filled with blood and sex, might just end in another murder.

"Emery sweetheart, maybe the next time when everything is settled."

She snarled, flashing her fangs. "No. You all baby me but I'm not a child. I want to remember what it feels like to have a cock inside me. The vibrator Maisie gave me isn't enough anymore. Please Theo, please Blair, I promise that I won't do what I did again. But he smelt so good and the throbbing between my legs was so strong."

Theo looked at Blair again and arched her brow, to which Blair mouthed back a name. "Silas."

Theo needed to go speak to the other Zayan to make sure he

was okay. However, first she had to deal with a horny Emery. They did not put this in the Suzerain handbook.

Crouching down in front of Emery, she rested her hands on Emery's bare knees. "Sweetie, you know we've talked about this. What happened to you was wrong...and even if Silas smelled good, you can't just think he wants to have sex with you."

Emery grinned. "Well, it felt like he did when I wrapped my hands around his cock."

Jesus, fucking Christ.

Theo let the power that made her Suzerain into her tone. "Emery. You won't touch Silas without his permission again. Go to your room and change your clothes."

Emery snarled and flashed her fangs. She pushed Theo's hands away and stormed from the room. Theo leaned forward and placed her head on the seat in front of her. She took a couple of deep breaths and then turned to look at Blair.

"Did she really go and try and give Silas a hand job?"

Blair nodded, sweeping the burgundy side of her hair off her shoulder. "Yup. He was asleep when she crept into his room and climbed into bed with him. He's worried everyone will think he took advantage."

Of course, he would. This was Silas. The brute of a man who was the gentlest soul. There was a connection between him and Emery, though the depths of that connection, Theo had no idea. Vampires sometimes took mates, and once you took a mate, only death could separate you. Theo wasn't interested in all that bullshit but knew that Silas was the kind of Zayan who would love a partner to call his own.

"Emery is technically an adult. Sometimes she might go off to cloud cuckoo land, which is understandable, but if she wants to have sex, I say we let her. Might do her mental health good to have sex that isn't forced upon her."

Theo asked Blair to go check on Emery, then went in search of Silas.

Instead, she happened upon an interesting interaction.

Valerian was standing just outside Maisie's lair, a grim expression on his face.

"I have done nothing to give you that impression."

Theo heard Maisie snort. "You practically stabbed my date with your death glare. There is nothing that says just because your blood made me a vampire that you can dictate who I hang out with. And for the record, normal people like to be touched."

Maisie slammed the door right in Valerian's face and he looked so shocked that Theo burst out laughing. Valerian turned to glare at her, a flush on his pale cheeks.

"I'm glad the fact that my Zayan fights me every step of the way amuses you."

"I just like seeing you riled up. When I was younger, I used to think that you were unrufflable. You're just used to having students that follow your every word like it's gospel."

Valerian arched a silver brow. "You didn't."

"I was just preparation for Maisie."

Valerian looked like he wanted to say more, but he started to head down the stairs.

"Hey Val?" Theo called after him, and he halted on the stairs. "If it gets on your nerves that some guy is hitting on Maisie, then you need to ask yourself why that is."

"It matters not."

Theo laughed. "Sure it doesn't. But as I'm already dealing with drama of a sexual nature, let me remind you that Maisie is old enough if you want to get her naked, but as your sort of kinda daughter, I don't want to know the details."

She left Valerian to his brooding, and climbed up the stairs to Silas' room. Theo could almost feel him stressing from outside the door. Lifting her knuckles to rap on the door, Theo waited a moment before she said. "Silas, it's me. I'm coming in."

Theo entered the room to see the Zayan sitting on the edge of his bed. The curtains were open slightly, throwing light onto his skin. Silas' room was one of the few rooms where the window was not tinted, so Silas could absorb the sunlight when he needed to.

It hurt him. So, it looked like Silas was punching himself.

He wore nothing but a pair of loose workout pants, showing off the ink that he had on his skin, done both before his rebirth as a vampire and after. He was hunched over, trying to make himself appear smaller as he lifted his head to look at Theo.

"I wouldn't have touched her." He ground out.

Theo closed the door behind her. "We know. We should have seen the signs. *I* should have. If it was any other vampire, then I would already have issued their death warrant. If any other vampire touched another without permission, they'd be dead right now."

"Don't. She didn't realize."

Theo sat down beside Silas on the bed. "I know. And it's okay to be attracted to her, Silas. Emery is beautiful. She sometimes laughs so easily that we forget the things that were done to her. She doesn't let just anyone even touch her, yet she trusts you to hold her."

Silas scrubbed a hand down his face. "It feels wrong. But Emery is the only one who does not think before touching me. I understand no one wants to cause me pain, but sometimes, I just want someone to touch me."

"And you want that to be Emery?"

Silas shrugged, getting up off the bed and walking to the window to look out it. "Is she alright?"

Theo laughed, which made Silas turn back to face her. "No. Little miss sassy is pissed that we are all trying to cock block her. She wants to go to the vamp night at the club. And told me and Blair she wanted to have sex."

Silas turned away again, and Theo knew that he must be at war with his own thoughts and emotions. It must be extremely hard for Silas, to feel human touch and the powers he has that makes his skin impenetrable means that the slightest touch, the ghost of a brush of fingers could be agony.

But if it was Theo, would she be able to go through her life devoid of touch. As much as the Scion could be a pain in her ass, she would hate to not know what a hug from Kannon was like. What it was like to have Blair dye her hair and feel the massage of her fingers as she did her thing. How much pain would she endure for the countless nights she had fallen to sleep in Kaan's arms, as a child and as an adult.

Hell, even the way Valerian would cup her cheek and say nothing when she did something to make him proud.

Those were things Theo would never give up even if it meant it caused her pain.

"Maybe," She began as she got to her feet. "Just maybe, we've been handling the downside to your powers all wrong. Maybe it's like how you were at the start with the sun."

"I'm not sure I follow." Silas admitted turning back to Theo.

Theo gave Silas a smile. "When you were first reborn, the sun was agony on your skin. Because the way your molecules fused. Over time, it hurt a little less. We fucked up, Silas. We stopped touching you so that it wouldn't hurt, when maybe we should have been touching you all along."

Silas' brows raised and that made Theo laugh. "Okay maybe that came out a little dirtier than intended. So, right now, I'm gonna give you a five second hug and then tomorrow we aim for six."

Theo didn't wait for Silas to argue the point, she just went over and wrapped her arms around his waist and rested her head against his chest. After five seconds, she stepped out of the embrace and looked up at Silas.

"You good?"

The Zayan nodded, his body still tense. "And what about Emery?"

Theo shrugged, walking to the door. "If you want her to stop, then you need to tell her. She doesn't understand subtly. But you either gotta draw the line and tell her that you see her as nothing more than a sibling, and that you aren't interested in sex with her or anything else, or decide that you want to see if there's more there. I can help if you want me to."

Theo opened the door and was about to head out when Silas said her name.

"Thank you. I was afraid I'd be blamed and cast out."

"Nah," Theo told him as she let her lips curve into a deeper grin. "Who the fuck would handle all my security? And all the bloody plants around this place? I think I'd be more replaceable than you would, Silas."

Theo's head was hurting as she left Silas to his thoughts, so instead of heading down to the main spaces to work, she went back toward her bedroom. Then at the last minute, she headed toward Kaan's room, scenting before she entered that her oldest friend was alone.

Kaan was sitting up in bed, shirtless with a tablet in his hands. Theo closed the door and climbed onto his silk bedding and slipped under the covers and then leaned against his shoulder.

"Bad day already?" Kaan asked as he nudged her with his shoulder after setting his tablet down to the side of the massive bed.

"I feel like a fraud!" Theo exclaimed.

"Most of us do, darling. Are you thinking in general, or has something specific triggered it today?"

Theo told him about everything that had happened, about Silas and Emery, then Valerian and Maisie. Kaan listened intently to Theo rambled on, with a blank expression.

"How the fuck can I be lecturing everyone on relationships?"

Kaan was quiet for a while, then when he spoke, Theo could hear the emotion in his voice. "You know how to be tough, Theo. You know how to be strong. But while it would make some people hard, you still have the capacity to be warm and loving. It's rather sickening actually."

Theo laughed, knowing that Kaan meant every word, even if he tried to pretend that he was aloof and uncaring to anyone but Theo. It was as much a defence mechanism as Theo did with her hair and clothing. They had learned from a young age, that clothes and hair, and pretending was all part of the gig, that being Paza meant putting on a show, of acting the role.

"I was going to wait to give these to you, but you look so sad, and I can't stand looking at your mopey face any longer." Kaan waited until Theo had sat up and he could reach into his bedside table and pulled out a box.

He handed it over to Theo and she opened it to see a brand-new pair of steampunk googles.

Theo grinned as she picked them up and looked them over before putting them back into the box, she put them gently on the other locker and gave Kaan a hug. "Thank you, those are epic."

Kaan gave her one of his rare genuine smiles, as he released against the headboard and let Theo hold him a little longer. They just stayed there, holding one another like they had for many a year.

Theo huddled on her cot and shivered, not from the cold but from fear. Valerian had been gone for a while, sent to fetch another Velesan and that meant that their training and care was to be undertaken by Nyx.

Today had been tough.

Nyx had her fighting with Eris in the morning and Keres in the afternoon. He had given the twins a human to feed from, but not Theo. She was bruised and battered by the time Nyx had grinned and told her that she needed to fight the twins, two on one.

He was punishing her for something that she didn't know...of that she was certain.

Kaan had been fighting a Russian Velesan, who had been lite and graceful, taking the vampire down in a few minimal steps. He'd asked Nyx to partner Theo in the fight and Nyx had sent him from the room.

At first, Kaan had not wanted to leave her. Theo pleaded with her eyes for him to go. It would be worse if he defied Nyx. She could not stand to see him hurt.

The blanket over Theo was lifted and Kaan slid in beside her, wrapping his arms around her and pulling Theo against him. They said nothing, just held each other, and in the darkness, Theo allowed herself a moment to cry, and to wonder if they would ever be free of this hell.

Blinking her eyes to rid herself of the memories, Theo said to Kaan. "I don't think I would have survived the Order without this. Without you."

"Right back at ya, darling." Kaan drawled, playing with the strand of her hair.

"Since I'm dishing out all this relationship advice, can I give you some?"

An exasperated sigh escaped Kaan's lips. "Do I have a choice?"

"Nope, but it's only cause I love you." Theo told him. "Let Kannon in. Stop pushing him to the point that he will do and find what he's looking for somewhere else. Talking to Silas this morning made me realize that in spite of all we went through, we came out a little less unscathed than some. Is whatever you're afraid of worth the risk of losing a man that could make you really happy?"

Kaan shifted out of the bed and went over to the wardrobe and took out a plain tunic. He didn't respond to Theo's words at first and then said very softly. "Theo, I love you, but you gotta let it go. I tried, once. And he rejected me. I will not beg him for affection. I have my pride."

That was news to Theo. She wanted to knock their two heads together.

"You want to tell me about it?" Theo asked him, watching as he turned and gave her his best charming smile.

"There is absolutely nothing to talk about."

Theo pursed her lips together and lifted her brows, but Kaan dismissed her with the wave of his hand. Slipping off the bed, she went over and gave him a quick hug, then grabbed her new goggles and headed out to make a second attempt to go to work.

 **MAX**

Another few days had passed without incident and Max was starting to feel twitchy. Or that's how Rían had described it when they had met for a drink last night. Max was also waiting for the results of his CT scan, ones that were due to come in any day now and he couldn't stop thinking about the things his mother had said.

He'd driven to the storage unit that held all the boxes of his mam and dad's possessions and went looking for anything that might give him a clue to the full extent of his mam's madness. He found all the old leather-bound books his mam used to make him read, as well as a few handwritten books in different languages.

Max had sat down in the middle of the storage unit for hours researching, had been about to give up when he knocked over a box and out fell a dozen or so leather covered notebooks. Crouching down to pick one up, Max flipped the page, recognised his mam's handwriting. He traced the curves with his fingertips, then began to read through the passages.

December 15, 1990

We almost had that Zayan. We did. But he managed to give us the slip. If Brendan hadn't of almost fallen as he jumped over the rooftops, I could have added the vampire to my tally. We'll get him and the rest of his Scion.

My time is running out. I need to enjoy each and every hunt for as long as I can. The chieftains are already trying to find a suitable match for me. Brendan too. Our numbers have been decimated by the vampires and I must do my duty and conceive the next generation of Cathainites.

I'm not sure I have what it takes to be a mother. I'm a hunter. It's in my blood.

What sort of man will accept that the hunt comes before everything else? What children would understand? And if you do feel some molecule of love toward a child, how do you raise them only to bring them into this life where death becomes a part of you.

Max's heart was pounding as he flipped through the pages, reading little parts about his mother and then when she had been introduced to his dad.

May 26, 1994

Elliot is an intelligent man. Handsome. He made me laugh. His career as an architect means that he can stay at home and take care of any children we might have. He understands my role, his role.

The negotiation went well. I was surprised at how easily he agreed to most of our conditions. He would take my surname. He would be responsible for raising the children. He only had two stipulations of his own. No affairs and at least two children. One child for the Cathainites, one for him.

That was a reasonable request.

Max closed the notebook. His mam had been suffering with those delusional thoughts for longer than he had suspected. How the hell had she manged to hide it for so long? He really wasn't sure if he wanted to read any more, especially if Aideen had written down her feelings toward her children. If it was bad, Max didn't want to know, and Shauna could never know that any of this shit ever existed.

Gathering up the notebooks, and putting them back in the box, Max had bent down to pick up the last one, only to see a sticky note with his name on it, in the same handwriting as in the notebooks.

His heart seemed to skip a beat as he opened the notebook to the first page and read the first page.

Max,

If you are reading this, my son, then I'm not around to explain it all to you. For that I am sorry. I knew the moment that you were placed on my chest that you were like me, you looked at me with serious eyes and I felt it, the power in your veins.
You must be confused. I was when my father explained it to me.

You are a descendant of the cathain like in the stories I told you.
It is your legacy to hunt vampires.
But not all the things you know of vampires are true.
A velesan can walk in sunlight.
A vayan cannot.

You have probably come across some already. You'll feel it in your gut, the pull.
I'll try and put as much knowledge as I can on paper, but if you have questions, ask your father. Elliot knows what you will become.
He can help you understand and prepare you.
Because as much as you will feel the urge to hunt vampires, they will also hunt you

Max had slammed the notebook shut. Fucking insanity. How the hell had his dad not seen this long before his wife had murdered him? How had he not seen it? Aideen had always seemed so rational, calm, but she had never appeared as crazy as all the fucking pages and pages of notebooks made her out to be.

He had gone to the storage unit in search of answers and all he had done was leave with more questions. Before he had left, Max had seen the antique trunk that had been in his mam's office and opened it, coughing at the dust. Instead of holding old books or scrolls, the trunk had been an array of weapons, ones that Max had assumed were collector's pieces.

Max had picked up the first weapon on the top and turned it over in his hands. It was an ornate Japanese sword, with kanji inscribed on the handle. It was the kind of piece you put in a display case so that everyone could admire it. The hilt had been heavy in his hand, and yet, it didn't feel odd to be holding it.

His gaze had dropped to the trunk, and he had dropped the sword. Slamming the trunk shut after seeing the array of finely crafted stakes peeking out from behind the metal.

Max left the storage unit, driving off toward the station when his phone rang.

His GP.

"Afternoon doc." He said in a way of greeting.

"Max, I've got your results." His doctor said, then started to go through the test results.

There was nothing wrong with his brain. He wasn't going mad.

Then what the fuck was happening to him?

He thanked his doctor and hung up midway through the doctor telling him that perhaps he should increase his visitations to his therapist. Sure, that would go down a threat with his therapist... telling her that his mother had told him that he was a descendant of an ancient Irish vampire hunter, and that despite getting the all-clear on his head scan, all the weird shit that was happening to him made him wonder if his mother was really even insane?

Max barked out a laugh as he pulled into the station, was about to get out of the car when his phone rang and surprise and panic coursed through his body. He pressed answer on the speaker.

"Shauna, what's wrong?"

His sister was crying down the phone and he could barely make out a word that she was saying. Max told her to take a breath and tell him what happened.

"Megan's dead. Someone killed her. I went to get her for dinner and, oh my god, Max, it's like an animal tore her apart."

Shit.

Mike came out of the station and Max pointed to the phone. His boss got into the car beside him but said nothing as Max concentrated on his sister.

"Shauna, have you called the Garda? Did you touch anything?"

"I called them before you and I only touched the door

handle. I wanted to check if Megan was alive, but I knew from all that blood that she couldn't be."

Shauna started to cry again as Max tore out of the station, Mike hanging onto the door as Max broke about every speed limit in Cork City, knowing that Megan Connolly lived in student accommodation near to University College Cork. He told Shauna to wait for the uniforms to show up and he'd be there in a few. Like Shauna, Megan had been doing an arts degree, but she was focusing on language and politics.

And now she was dead because of him.

"Might not be the same guy."

Max shot Mike a skeptical glare. They both knew that the murderer they were hunting had killed his sister's best friend. The killer had chosen a victim close to his sister. Did the killer know that Max was hunting him? And how the fuck was Megan connected to The Player's Lounge?

It could have been Shauna. It could have been her murder you're off to investigate.

Mike was on the phone to Rían, who immediately asked if Shauna was okay. Mike told her that they were waiting for visual confirmation, but that Max had spoken to her. Rían told Max to be Shauna's brother first before he went full Detective on her, to which Max told him to fuck right off and get his ass to the crime scene instead of playing Doctor Phil.

The moment Max ground to a halt outside the student accommodation, he was out of the car and jogging up the steps to the main doors. He ignored all the crying students gathered in the lobby and took the stairs two at a time. He needed to see that Shauna was actually unharmed...

He rounded the corner and didn't even flash his badge as the Garda making sure no one got on to the floor nodded, letting him through. His gaze darted through the halls, which were eerily quiet. Where the fuck was Shauna?

Max paused at the door to Megan's room. He knew which one it was because the company he hired to watch over Shauna had given him a blow by blow of every single place Shauna frequented. The door to the apartment across the way from

Megan's was ajar and Max turned to see Shauna sitting on the edge of the bed, a Garda keeping watch over her.

She lifted her head and saw him, launching off the bed. "Oh my god, Max."

Max wrapped his arms around her, let her cry into his chest as he just held her. He needed to go check out the scene before anyone else fucked it up, but he was trying to be Shauna's brother. She could go back to hating him tomorrow.

The hunt comes before everything else.

Max sucked in a gulp of air, his mam's words slamming into his mind. Shauna lifted her head and Max let her step away. He glanced over his shoulder and then back at his sister.

"I'm sorry you had to see that. You feel up to telling me a little about what Megan was up to last night?"

She nodded, her face red and puffy. "She had a date last night. She's been seeing this new guy. Older. She went out with him last night, but I had an assignment that was due this morning I needed to finish so I stayed home. We always check in after a night out, just to make sure everything's okay. And she checked in Max. She checked in so she should be OK."

Max had been the one to tell Shauna to do just that, knowing the first twenty-four of any crime were the most important hours to finding someone alive. He felt a sense of pride, however, it was eclipsed by the guilt that Shauna would now never scrub the image of her dead friend from her mind.

"She texted me at two to say she was home and would see me for dinner. So, I came over as planned and that's when I found her. I only touched the door handle and walked into the room. I told you that already, didn't I?"

Max gave her a small smile. "It's good to remind me. You know who this new boyfriend was? Have you guys met?"

Shauna shook her head. "No. I asked but Megan kept putting it off. She said she wanted to enjoy the newness and the sex before everyone knew about them. Because of the age gap. Like he was older than you. But she promised me I would meet him on Wednesday."

Max filed that information away for later as he leaned in and kissed his sister on top of her head. "I'm gonna have a Garda take you home and stay there until I come home later. I promise you that I will find out what happened to Megan."

"I can help." Shauna said with a steely determination.

No, you can't. You'll only get in the way of the hunt.

"I can't do my job if I'm worried about you, Shauna. Please don't fight me on this. Go home. Let me do my job."

Shauna looked like she was going to argue with him, but Mike came in and with the calmness Max had always found irritating, he managed to convince Shauna that it was for the best and Max would work best if he wasn't worrying about her.

A thought popped into his head and he put his hand on Shauna's hand. "Do you know where Megan was going last night with the boyfriend?"

"Ya," Shauna said, looking at the closed door across the way. "The Player's Lounge. Megan's parents gave her gold standard membership. That's where she met him. We were supposed to go to the vampire night on Wednesday and she was gonna introduce me."

And all roads led back to The Player's Lounge.

"Max."

Max had already started toward the door of Megan's room when Shauna called him. "Her parents shouldn't have to see her like that."

"Rían will take good care of her. I promise."

Max waited until Shauna had been escorted from the floor, glancing at Mike, who handed him booties, and nothing else. "Go, do your thing. If Kelly asks, I ordered you to put on the suit. But we all know you don't listen."

Mike was trying to alleviate the tension and it did the trick as Max chuckled before putting on his blue booties, adding gloves because even though he hated the suit, he knew what was important. Pushing open the door, he stepped inside and left it open so he could talk through things with Mike.

The room reminded him of his room in boarding school. It was an open plan room with a bathroom to the side. Designed for single occupancy the room had one desk that had books in different languages piled on top of one another. A framed photo of Megan and Shauna was positioned off to the side. Taped to the wall was a picture of Cork City at night that was breath-taking, hand drawn in pencil and charcoal. It had Shauna's initials at the end of the drawing.

Megan's mobile phone was plugged in to charge. Max would look at that later to see if he could find any clues to the mysterious boyfriend. It had been a theory of his that the killer was a regular at The Player's Lounge, and from what Shauna had told him, his hunch was right.

Nothing seemed out of place in the room, well other than the body. He closed his eyes, letting himself just feel through his thoughts and assessments before he turned to look at Megan. As his eyes landed on the body, Max pushed the image of the young woman who had been eating breakfast in his house just a few days ago, and focused on the body like it was any other murder.

The victim had been posed much like the victims at Mill Lane. The victim was naked with her throat slashed, and blood smeared all down her throat. There was purplish bruising to the parts of her neck that hadn't been staged with blood.

She had similar bruising on her thighs, and her breasts. Her torso was clawed, and it reminded Max of the woman who had clawed at his face. The marks weren't the same, but Max assumed that the killer was trying to make them look at the woman he'd fought with and steer away from him.

The victim's heart had been ripped from her chest. Max leaned in to take a closer look. It wasn't a clean cut by any means, but the way the gap was, it struck Max that the heart might have been removed by a utensil not too dissimilar to what Rían used during an autopsy. She was holding her own heart in her left hand and Max could see the indentation of teeth on the organ.

The killer had bitten the heart like some of his other victims.

Her knees had been bent, most likely after she had died, but Rían would confirm that. Like the other victims, she had an object shoved inside her vagina. The killer had posed her with her right hand on the end of the object, like the victim had done this to herself. This was covered in blood. Max had seen something similar this morning in his mother's trunk.

Realization dawned.

The killer had penetrated her with a wooden stake.

Anger boiled in his blood. What the fuck did it all mean?

Max swallowed down his rage and looked at the victim's face. Her make up was smeared, her face tear stained as her vacant eyes looked at Max, as if they were begging him to save her. The victim's lips were parted, and Max tilted his head.

There was something in her mouth.

Max went over to the small vanity and looked for some tweezers. He found a pair, gave them a little wipe with his glove and then went back to the body. He extracted what turned out to be a piece of paper gently so as not to disturb the position of the body. Last thing he needed was for Rían to bust his balls for messing with his crime scene.

Again.

Max held the piece of paper and unfolded it carefully.

The message was typed, like the killer didn't want his handwriting to give him away. Rían had told him once that someone's handwriting was almost as identifiable as a fingerprint. It told you so much about a person.

What did his mother's handwriting say about her?

Shoving that thought away, Max looked at the message, written in Romanian, but it roughly translated to: The hunter that chases two rabbits never catches one.

The killer was taunting him. That much was evident. He was chasing two rabbits instead of focusing on catching the one he needed to. He needed to hunt one killer instead of worrying about others hiding secrets.

He heard someone clearing their throat, shifted his gaze to see Mike standing in the hall.

"Talk to me, Max."

Certainty settled in his chest.

"I need to talk to Theo Caden. I need to get inside The Player's Lounge. The killer is inside her house."

THEO

Theo heard the commotion in the hallway as she was making the final preparation plans for their vampire night. She heard a scuffle, then a grunt as she wondered who the fuck was fighting outside her goddamn office this close to closing time. All she wanted to do was go home, soak in a tub for an hour, then go to bed.

Maybe feed since it had been a couple of days since she had last done so. She'd decided against feeding from Simon again and instead fed from one of the other women. Her horniness was less likely to take over when feeding from a woman, since Theo wasn't that way inclined.

Taking a second before she opened her office door, she didn't bother to mask the surprise in her face at what she was seeing.

A certain Detective Sergeant had Simon pinned to the wall, his fingers wound tight into the t-shirt that Simon was wearing that said The Player's Lounge on the front and security on the back. Simon wasn't a small guy, and security was literally his job, but Max was making him look like an amateur.

Simon glanced in her direction, his face red with embarrassment. "I tried to stop him."

There was nothing Simon could have done against a Cathainite in the middle of a hunt and from the rage in Max's brown eyes, he was most definitely on the hunt, even if he didn't know it.

"Detective Sergeant if you have finished man-handling my staff, then I assume it's me you've come to talk to. Let him go."

Theo could see Max tense at the order, however he let Simon go and stormed past Theo, walking right into her office. Simon made to follow, but Theo held up her hand. "I've got this. Go and tell Kaan that I'm having a meeting with the Detective, but I'll still be leaving with him."

Simon looked like he wanted to argue. See this was why Theo had decided to stop feeding from Simon. He was getting expectant. Arrogant. And it was a massive turn off. He'd been around vampires long enough to know that food was food.

Now, he'd have to chase his highs somewhere else.

Theo closed the door of her office as Simon continued to look at her. A moment later, Theo heard the elevator come up and the ping as the doors closed. Right, dickhead number one dealt with, now to deal with the other one.

Theo looked over to see Max standing with his back to her, tension in his shoulders as he starred at the sword on display behind her desk. Her father's sword. Theo had snuck into the castle after her father had died, when her uncle Radu had ascended to the throne. Her uncle had been using her father's sword as a deterrent, a warning, but Theo wanted it as a reminder.

"My mother used to collect artifacts like that. Yesterday I found a load of them in a truck. Not sure why I'm telling you this."

Theo wasn't sure either, and yet, she liked that Max felt like he could trust him with something that was obviously deeply personal to him, even when he really shouldn't.

Theo came to stand beside him, looked up at her father's sword and gave Max an honest answer...well as honest as she could without telling him that the sword that he was admiring used to belong to the man the world knew as Vlad the Impaler and she was his illegitimate daughter that most noted as unknown in the ancestry.

"My father wasn't present in my life. He was in politics. My mother died not long after I was born. I grew up in a sort of foster home with Kaan. I was obsessed with knowing about where I came from. Spent hours researching. That sword came from that obsession. Like, it's probably not authentic but the guy who sold it to me told me it dates back to a region of Romania in the 1400's."

Max glanced at her and back to the sword. "Back to the reign of Vlad the Impaler."

This time it was Theo who looked at Max. "Secret history buff?"

Max chuckled darkly as he ran his fingers through his hair. "My mother used to make me do extra study of history. Languages too. I'm handy to have at a pub quiz."

Theo snorted a laugh. "Good to know. So, what has you man-handling my staff at this late hour? Or early depending how you see it."

Max turned his dark gaze back to the sword. "My sister's best friend was murdered last night. She was here before she died. Had a gold standard subscription so my sister said."

Theo's heart sank and her stomach rolled. "Who was it?"

"Megan Connolly."

Shit. Theo knew the girl. She was a great student who loved to come and let loose. She liked an older guy, one who took control. That was her kink. Well, that and her fascination with vampires. Theo was certain that Megan didn't know that vampires were real, but she did have sex with some of the vampire wannabes. The ones with the fake teeth and the make up to appear paler.

Then it dawned on Theo that the girl with the dark hair and the tattoos who Megan brought as her guest a few times must be Max's sister. His sister too was obsessed with vampires, though she had never indulged in sex with any pretend vamps that Theo knew of...and Theo certainly wasn't about to tell her big brother that.

"Max came home to find that his mother had gone mad and murdered his father by driving a leg of a chair through his heart. The records state that Aideen De Barra, was raving about her husband Elliot being a vampire."

Ah now Shauna's interest in vampires made sense.

"I knew Megan." Theo said honestly, folding her arms across

her chest. "She used to practice her Romanian with me. She had a real gift for languages. Damn, what a fucking waste."

"My sister found her body."

Theo reached out and touched her hand to Max's arm. "Ah shit, Max. I'm sorry. She must be traumatized."

Max sighed and Theo took her hand away. "I've tried to shelter her from how fucked up the world is. I did my best to hide certain things from her and now a killer knows I'm closing in on him and in order to throw me off the hunt, he's targeted my sister's friend."

The hunt.

He was even starting to sound like a fucking Cathainite.

Max turned to face her, his face an emotionless mask though his eyes burned with anger. "I know that you've been deflecting that the killings have nothing to do with you or this club. But you're wrong. I read the sign on my way in: Welcome to The Player's Lounge - Tell us your nightmares and fantasies."

Theo shook her head. "It's a catchy tagline."

"But it's the truth. You indulge in people's fantasies here. You let them pretend for a night that they can be whoever. The killer's fantasies were awoken in this club."

Theo held his gaze in silence so Max continued.

"The house on Mill Lane. That was the killer acting on his fantasies. The people there were free. They fucked who they wanted. He probably tried to get in on the sex and they rejected him. The security guard had his suspicions and he died because of it. And the girl in the alley was murdered because she played the part of you in the fantasies of those who came here but knew they would never get to touch you."

Theo swallowed hard. It had occurred to her exactly what Max was saying but that was when she thought that it was all a game Nyx was playing, and now that she was certain that it wasn't, Theo didn't have a clue who the killer was.

"The killer is either one of your hundred or so staff, or a punter who comes to the club and playing pretend isn't good enough anymore."

"You seem so certain that the killer has a hard on for me."

Max jerked his head up toward the sword and said in perfect Romanian. "The hunter that chases two rabbits never catches one."

"I think the killer is locked in a fantasy where he wants to or believes he's a vampire. Things that were done to the bodies. Bite marks. He likes the idea of being immortal. Of the status and beauty, he thinks it will bring him. The power. It's like an addiction now and I think tomorrow night's vampire night will be the best chance to catch him."

Theo perched herself on the edge of her desk, looked up at Max. She shouldn't be as transfixed by his assessment. She shouldn't be as aroused by it. "What makes you think that?"

Max shifted his weight, then ran his fingers through his hair. "He won't be able to help himself. The illusion. The theatre of it all. People pretending to be children of the night. The scents and sounds and the adrenaline will make him brave. He'll think it's camouflage. That all of the fantasies going on around him will allow him to indulge. But it's what will give him away."

Max didn't know it, but his eyes had darkened, like the thought of hunting his prey was an aphrodisiac. Most guards wouldn't think like Max, but he wasn't an ordinary guard. No, Max De Barra was one of the strongest Cathainites she had ever seen, and the motherfucker didn't even know it.

"He'll be hungry. Megan's murder won't have satisfied him. It was too quick. He didn't have enough time to savior it. Megan was an inconvenience. He played at being her boyfriend, but she would have gotten in the way of what he plans for tomorrow night."

Realization dawned on Theo. "You think he's gonna come for me?"

Max nodded his head. "The ultimate high. The ultimate fantasy. His vampire queen who has awakened the darkness inside of him."

"That's oddly specific, Max. Looks like you put a lot of thought into that."

Max took his phone out of his pocket and brought up a video of Theo from last year. It was the Halloween special night, and the theme had been vampire court. Prior to the event, ticket holders were sent envelopes of the part they would play. Theo had indeed played the vampire queen.

Blair had done her hair and makeup that night. Her hair had been dyed a blood red that night, her lips painted the same colour. The corset she wore pushed her breasts up and out. The skirt of the dress was poofed out. The dress had been Theo's, one she had actually worn to a party back when her father was still alive. She just hadn't worn the petticoat that usually accompanied it.

In her hand was a goblet, the liquid in it coloured to look like blood. As she made her way down the stairs, those dressed as members of her vampire Kiss, bowed to her. She playfully kissed Blair's lips, then her throat before lifting her face and flashing her fangs.

"That was the moment he became fixated on you."

"Really?"

"You look regal." Max told her, his dark eyes drinking her in as he slid the phone away. "You look out of reach. Forbidden. Fuckable. You made every man and woman wonder about what it would be liked to be fucked by you. I'd say not a single man at the party needed Viagra that night because they only had to look at you and get hard."

Theo's skin felt flushed. She wanted to know if Max felt that way about her. If she asked him that, would he take her right now, hard on her desk? Would he bite her back if she bit him?

Christ on a bike, it was fucking warm in here.

"You want to use me as bait?"

Max shrugged, taking a step away, as his tongue flicked out to wet his lips. "No. I want to use me as bait. He knows I'm coming for him. He thinks he can outsmart me. I need his focus on me and not on you."

Theo frowned. She hadn't been expecting that but how the hell did Max expect to shift the killer's attention from her to him. Max reached around and rubbed the back of his neck.

"To do that, I do need your help."

"Tell me." Theo said, resting her hands on the edge of the table.

"You just have to pretend you like me."

Theo laughed, crossing her legs in front of her. "How's that gonna help?"

"You need to pretend that you want to fuck me." He said in a gravelly tone that clenched areas of her body that she really didn't want to be clenching as Max continued.

"He thinks he can get your attention tomorrow and tell you all the things he has done to impress you. But he will be pissed off if he thinks that he missed his chance because you're focused on me. He will want to take me out to get to you."

Theo narrowed her gaze, adrenaline in her veins as she said. "So, you want me to pretend to want to fuck you so he tries to kill you."

"Something like that." Max mumbled and Theo heard his heart beat a little faster.

Ah, so she wasn't the only one who wasn't repulsed by the idea.

But she was also gonna have some fun with it.

Theo pushed off her desk and walked round to sit on her chair. She ran her gaze over Max, then tilted her head. "Okay, I can play pretend. I like a good role play. But we have got to do something about your outfit."

Max looked down at his clothes. "What's wrong with my clothes?"

Theo waved her hand. "It screams Garda. And not enough leather. How do you feel about leather pants?"

"I'm not wearing leather pants, Theo."

"So, I'm guessing that's a no to a leather collar and a leash? No wait, it's handcuffs that gets you going."

Max gave her a death stare, and Theo bit the inside of her mouth not to laugh. "You're taking the piss out of me?"

"Of course I am. You are tense as fuck. But I was totally serious about the leather pants. And no shirt. You're waxed right?"

Max's glare got even worse as Theo dismissed the comment

with the wave of her hand. "Doesn't matter. Women go crazy for the Roy Kent chest hair nowadays." She lifted her eyes from his chest to his eyes. "And the eyebrows. Defo the Roy Kent effect."

Max left quickly after that, like he was fully convinced that Theo would whip out her measuring tape and start measuring the inseam of his pants. From what Theo had seen in her appraisal, the Bowie Bulge would be on show if she managed to get Max in a tight enough pair of leather trousers.

She told Max to come by the club around seven so Kaan could get him dressed. He had cried off until she told him that Kaan wouldn't force him into anything he wasn't comfortable in, but he had to look the part of someone who actually wanted to be a vampire...or a vampire's lover.

Theo was grinning when Max had grunted and left the same way he had come in, like a fucking storm. She'd have to warn Kaan to keep the actual vampires out of Max's way, least they catch on to what he was, what he could be.

If he ever found out the truth of what she was, then it would be curtains.

It would be kill or be killed.

Theo spun round in her chair and looked up at her father's sword. The last time she had used it, the last time she had bathed it in blood was killing a Cathainite. She had been in London, looking for Kaan after he'd gone off and made no contact. He'd been in one of his dark moods and that usually took him to the streets of London where flesh was bought and sold.

Theo closed her eyes, thinking back to that night almost a decade ago.

Theo ran through the almost abandoned streets, her hair thumping across her back as she did. The Cathainite was close, too fucking close and while he was prepared to kill her in front of humans, Theo didn't have that luxury.

One look at her and they would scream vampire.

She'd been searching for Kaan for a whole bloody week and still hadn't found him.

No one seemed to bat an eyelid as she raced through the streets, sword in hand. But considering most of them were drunk or high, they probably thought they were imagining the sword wielding ginger running about the place.

Theo ducked down one street only to find it was a dead end when she reached the end of the cobbled path. A rumble of laughter sent her whirling round. At the mouth of the alley stood one of the Cathainites. Their paths had crossed many a time. But Theo had managed to slip his tail many times before.

Not tonight though.

"Daughter of Tepes. A fine kill to add to my collection."

"Come now, Brendan. You've survived longer than most. Don't mock death when it's this close to you."

The Cathainite lunged forward, his long yew stick no match for her sword. Theo sliced out as he came near, then cut the wood in two. Brendan now had two weapons. He backed off slightly and Theo just wanted it done.

She closed her eyes and used her power to astral project behind the man, wasting no time in slicing her sword right across his neck. Theo had already called her astral self back before his head bounced off the cobbles.

She barely spared him a second glance as she took off to continue her search for Kaan.

There might come a time when she and Max faced off in some darkened alley, enemies by fate. But unlike her and Kaan, there would be no way around it. And Theo knew that it would be her place to show the inexperienced Cathainite why vampires truly did own the night.

MAX

hen Max arrived at The Player's Lounge at a quarter to seven, and the big burly security guard Silas Orlov grunted as he led Max into the elevator. They rode the journey in silence until the doors opened and Silas told him that Kaan was waiting for him. Max's stomach had been twisted in knots all day and the moment he had arrived at The Player's Lounge the feeling had intensified.

It hadn't helped that Shauna had been upset about her friend and was shouting at Max, calling him constantly wondering why he hadn't caught the killer yet. He had a headache that was probably down to tension and down to lack of sleep.

While the killer was in his thoughts all the time, Theo was also at the forefront of his mind. He'd known she was messing with him last night about the clothes and that, but he had forced himself to make a hasty exit because he was seconds away from doing something stupid like kissing her.

Figures it would be the serial killer's object of desire that ignited something in Max that he hadn't felt before in his entire life. He'd been attracted to women before. He'd had his share of one-night stands, and he'd been with Vanessa a while, but the mundaneness felt boring.

Nothing about Theo Caden would be fucking boring.

Kaan Sydin was standing inside his office, a glass in his hand as he beckoned Max inside with his free hand, a smirk on his face. Max took a moment to consider that Kaan might take this opportunity to ensure Max made a fool of himself and he hoped like hell that Theo would have told him not to.

The man himself was dressed in leather pants that clung to

his lower half like a second skin. He had a crimson button-down shirt tucked into the waistband of his pants. The sleeves were rolled up to the elbows, and the buttons undone enough to show off the golden brown of his skin tone. His eyes had a smoky look to them that he'd seen Shauna wear on occasions, but this was more deliberate, more pronounced and it darkened the colour of his eyes to an almost black that immediately reminded Max of the woman that attacked him.

Max wasn't too sure but it also looked like Kaan was wearing lipstick.

Running his eyes over Max, Kaan said in a lazy drawl. "I can see why Theo wanted me to dress you. You'd stick out like a sore thumb. Take off your clothes."

Max arched a brow. "What are ya dressing me in?"

The other man laughed, the sound of it brushing against his skin like a caress and something inside Max made him clench his fists. Kaan stopped laughing and spared just a momentary glance at Max's hands before striding to the rack of clothing with the fluid grace of a dancer.

"Don't look so worried. Tonight is not the night to make a fool of you, Detective Sergeant. We want this killer caught as much as you do. I don't like Theo being in danger. You have nothing to fear from me tonight."

That felt suspiciously like an underhanded threat and when Max pointed it out to Kaan, the other man shrugged and just replied. "Not a threat, handsome. More like a promise. If you do something that gets Theo hurt then we will be having more than just a conversation."

Max just snorted in reply, because as much as the threat made him defensive, he couldn't blame the man for wanting to protect his friend. He'd do the same to protect the people he cared about. It might be a short list, but he would do it.

Max kicked off his trainers and slipped his hoody and tee over his head. He left the pants on for now, glad that he left most of his stuff in the car. Mike had wanted to send more undercovers with him into the club. Max had told him it was a bad idea. That these people who frequented the club knew who the other patrons were and the only reason they wouldn't be suspicious of Max was because Theo would be with him. Instead, his boss and the team were set up across the road waiting to catch the killer if he ran.

The thought of chasing the killer caused him to involuntary shiver and Kaan glanced at him.

"Cold, Detective Sergeant?"

Max shook his head. No, he wasn't bloody cold. He was getting excited about chasing the killer if he ran. He was thinking of letting him run just so Max could hunt him down. Imagining it made Max's body flush with heat, and he felt like he was starving.

This was insanity, right?

Kaan handed him a pair of pants that looked suspiciously like leather and when Max frowned, Kaan sighed impatiently. "Don't give me that look. They are jeans that just *look* like leather. They will allow you to move freely but give the appearance that you dressed for Theo."

Max was still frowning as he yanked down his own jeans and then pulled on the pants, surprised when he realized that Kaan hadn't been lying to him. He felt Kaan watching him as he fastened the button on the pants and slid the zipper up.

Lifting his gaze, Max regarded Kaan, that smirk still curling his lips.

"What?" Max asked, bristling at the attention.

"Nothing," replied Kaan, as he riffled through the rail, turning away from Max. "Would you be uncomfortable if I said that the pants look great on you, and that it's a shame we couldn't get you to reconsider about the leather?"

After finishing his question, Kaan turned to face him and handed him a black round neck t-shirt. Max pulled it on, and it was a little snugger for his taste, but Kaan was still looking at him and Max shrugged his shoulders.

"Uncomfortable is the wrong word. I don't care if you think my ass looks great, Kaan. That shit doesn't bother me. The whole vampire role play nights don't bother me. It's the son of a bitch killing women and mutilating their bodies that annoys the fuck out of me. Killing for personal gratification or whatever, that makes me angry."

Kaan held his gaze for a moment and then came over, paused, and held up a brush. "May I?"

When Max asked him what he was doing with the makeup, Kaan told him he was only contouring the side of his neck so the veins would stand out, and any revellers playing the part of vampires would notice it. Max let Kaan do his thing, then also let him put a powder on his face to make him appear paler.

"It's to give the appearance that you've been drunk from. That Theo has taken a bite out of you and your blood sustains her. It's all about fattening up the story."

Well, at least that was what Kaan said when he put some fake blood on the nape if his neck and did some marks that looked like the bite marks on the victims. Max was looking at himself in the mirror, surprised at just how well Kaan had been able to make him look like a vampire's blood bank.

His face was pale, making his eyes look sunken into his head. The pulse at his neck was definitely standing out more. His chest seemed broader, his waist slimmer. Max finished off his vampire lover outfit by slipping his feet into boots and then he sat down to lace them up.

Kaan seemed pleased with his efforts and Max told him he'd done a good job, and asked why Kaan didn't do this sort of thing for a living. That movies and TV studios would kill for this effortless skill.

The other man looked at him for a moment, like he was trying to figure out if Max was bullshitting him. Kaan drained his drink, then leaned against the wall. "This is just a bit of fun. I love what I do. When I first learned how do some of the stuff, it was to help victims cover up bruises. Some of the staff here, they've had hard lives. We do what we can until they ask for help."

Max filed that information away for a later date. Was this one of the things Theo was hiding from him? What other secrets lurked inside the walls of The Player's Lounge? What skeletons were buried under the floorboards?

The elevator opened and Theo strode out and Max stood up

to get a better look at her. Gone were the steampunk outfits she liked to wear, though the dress did have small details that could be steampunk. She wore a dress of black and red that seemed to make her look even more ethereal, though Max was sure that was the wrong way to describe her because she looked dangerous as much as she looked beautiful.

The dress was corseted that pushed her breasts upward, the collar of the dress wrapped around her neck, with blood-red glass-like little droplets dangling across the swell of her breasts, making them a focal point, and Max dipped his gaze for a moment, before running his eyes over her again.

Knee high boots clung to her toned legs, making them seem longer. The dress flowed out at the back but was cut short at the front. The laces on the boots were the same blood-red as the droplets at her breasts. The heels of her boots made no sound as Theo came further into the room. Her earrings matched the droplets.

Gold and red decorated her eyes, and she was wearing contacts that made her eyes appear red. She had kept her orange hair; the mass of orange was pinned back off her face in an old-fashioned style. Strands of it had been strategically pulled from the hairstyle to appear as if they had fallen out.

Her lips were painted a crimson and black, making them look bigger and even more seductive. Max's mind began to wonder, and he wondered what it would be like to kiss her dressed like this, to play the part she wanted him to play. And he couldn't stop imagining her on her knees before him, this stunning vampire queen as she unzipped him and took him into her hot, wet mouth.

He bit back the groan in his throat as Theo came in, walked over to him, and gripped his chin. His heart was racing as Theo inspected his neck, then grinned at Kaan. "Not bad."

Kaan chuckled. "I had little to do with your Max. Most of my efforts were spent on you today, Theo, darling. You'll cause uproar in that dress."

"Here's hoping." Theo replied, smiling herself before she turned back to Max. "You sure about this?"

Max nodded, his mouth dry as Kaan declared that his work was done, and he was off. Theo waited until they were alone, and she glanced over him, her sinful lips curling into a smug smile as she took in his pants, before bringing her eyes back to his.

"I still think the leather pants would have looked better, but Kaan did a good job with the jeans and tee."

"I look like an amateur compared to you." Max heard himself say, taking a step closer to Theo, feeling like a magnet was pulling him to her. The churning in his stomach was still there, but it was muted by the overwhelming desire he felt.

Something flashed in Theo's eyes, and she retreated a step. Max shoved down his disappointment and focused on the task at hand. When this was wrapped up and the killer was caught, he could go back to his life and forget all about Theo Caden and the secrets she was keeping.

Max knew it was a lie, however he told himself that anyways.

"Before we do this," Theo started, placing her hands on her hips, a stern expression on her face. "You might be here in an official capacity, but only to find the killer. There are innocent people here who have come to live out their fantasies. They can fuck who they want once everyone is a consenting adult."

Max folded his arms across his chest and listened.

"These people trust me. Trust this place. This is my world, and you are here because I allowed it. This is a place for pushing the limits, for succumbing to pleasure and wants and needs. People will be acting as vampires. There will be biting. There will be fucking. If you think any of this is going to mess with your head, then say now and we call the whole thing off."

There will be biting.

The killer was fond of biting his victims and that might be the place where he would linger, watching couples behaving like real vampires. That's where he needed to be.

"Is there somewhere in particular that people would go to be bitten?" Max asked, studying Theo as her eyes darted to his neck before she turned away from him.

So, Theo liked to bite...

Max felt his pulse quicken at the thought of Theo nipping at his pulse, and erotic images popped into his head.

"The basement level. It's set up for tonight to be like the nightclub from Blade."

Max arched a brow. "You gonna have blood fucking sprinklers too?"

Theo laughed and Max felt his lips curve into a smile. "You continue to surprise me, Max. Not that far but the lights will be dimmed as much as possible. There are alcoves for the illusion of privacy, but we have cameras just in case anyone tries to take more than is offered."

"We need to be down there. That's where the killer will be. And besides, if he thinks you are taking me down to have your wicked way with me, it will rightly piss him off."

Theo nodded her head, then held his gaze, which felt weird considering her eyes were red. "Okay. I need to know how far you want to pretend. I'm gonna have to act possessive. Touch you. No matter what books you read or movies you see, vampires are possessive of those they think of as theirs. You'll have to act your ass off, Max."

Max didn't reply, because he didn't want Theo to know just how much he wanted her to touch him. He wanted her hands on him, her mouth, the feel of her skin under his touch. He craved it.

Theo cleared her throat, then glanced at the clock over his head. It was almost nine and he watched as Theo closed her eyes for a moment, then opened them again. "Showtime."

Max shook out his body and fell into step beside Theo as they entered the lift and went downward. They stood beside each other in the elevator, inches from each other until Max asked. "Do you have pretend fangs?"

Theo turned to face him and when she grinned at him, Max saw that she was wearing very sharp looking fangs. He wondered what they would feel like on his skin. Was this what the killer wore when he was tearing shreds out of his victims?

Max tilted his head as Theo ran her tongue over the points, then they shifted inside her mouth, leaving only normal human teeth. He was fascinated by them, by her. He wanted to run his finger along the points.

"Magic, Detective." Theo said with a wink. "Common fakes can make you sound lispy and Kaan tells me that it's very hard to give a blowjob with the cheap ones."

Max barked out a laugh and he realized Theo was making him laugh to ease the tension. He rolled his eyes angled his body to face Theo. "Tell me what you need me to do. This is your world."

"Since you dismissed my collar and leash idea, when we walk out to the top of the stairs, I'm going to put my hand on the back of your neck. That screams possession. Those playing vampires will bow. At the end of the stairs someone will present a tray with a goblet, you will take it and hand it to me."

Max nodded, committing the instructions to memory.

"I'll lean in and press my lips to your pulse. Close your eyes. It will look as if you are trying to hide your desire. The crowd will eat it up."

Like he needed to pretend that he desired her.

"We will go to the "Royal" area, where I will sit, and you will sit at my feet. Touch me. Focus on me, and we act like we want to rip each other's clothes off. If your hunch is right, then the killer should make himself known."

Max was about to ask her more when the doors to the elevator pinged, Theo rolled her shoulders, lifted her head, and then placed a warm, feminine hand on the nape of his neck, and he shivered. He could feel the calluses on her palm. He felt the vibration from the music a second before the doors opened.

Quiet descended upon the heaving floor, the music halting as Theo stepped out, Max moving when she did. They paused at the top of the stairs as Theo stood for a moment at the top of the stairs, gave his nape a gentle but firm squeeze and then began to descend the stairs. True to her word, those dressed as vampires bowed as Theo came down the stairs.

Max scanned the room, saw the lust and desire on other people's faces, but he couldn't blame them. Theo really and truly was the Queen of The Player's Lounge and this performance, this spectacle just proved it to Max. He'd try and enjoy it, the pretence that he belonged to Theo, but that would go better if the cramping in his stomach would give it a rest for one night.

They reached the final step as Max grabbed the goblet off the tray that was placed in front of him, handing it off to Theo. Their fingers grazed and Theo licked her lips. Max could feel his heart fucking hammering against his chest, the pulse in his neck beating in time with it.

Max angled his head to give Theo better access to his throat, then closed his eyes like she had told him as he felt her breath on his skin, his palms itching to touch her.

His body was hard long before her hot lips closed over his pulse.

THEO

Bite him. Taste him. Fuck him.

Theo was down for letting the horny bitch in her head do just that to Max. This was a terrible idea. This was an awful, awful idea. She could tell from the scent of Max that he was turned on by all of it, by her. She should have called it all off when they were in Kaan's dressing room, but Theo had wanted to see how Max would react to all the theatrics.

He'd taken to the task like any human who wanted to serve a vampire. When he had angled his head to give her more access, her gums had throbbed, and she wanted to sink her fangs into his flesh and taste him.

It was sheer madness that she wanted the one man in this entire building with the power to kill her.

Closing her mouth over his racing pulse, Theo bit back a moan, but couldn't stop herself from flicking her tongue over that delicious flesh. Max's hand landed on her hip, squeezing hard, but Theo just sucked a little, enough to leave a faint mark on his skin.

When she reluctantly pulled back, Max was looking at her with an intensity that made her body clench and need claw at her stomach. Tearing her eyes from his, Theo placed her hand on his neck again and strutted toward the Royal area to see Kaan already lounging in there. He'd unbuttoned his shirt a little more, and Theo could see he'd put some gold shimmer on his torso.

No wonder Kannon was looking at him like he wanted to devour him.

Kaan got to his feet and held his hand out to Theo to help her take her own seat. She lowered herself down, then inclined her head to Blair who was behind the decks, and the music started up again, Theo almost grinning as Tiësto's *We Own the Night*, blared from the speakers and cheers rose among the crowd.

Theo fanned out her dress, Max having lowered himself on to the floor in front of her. His eyes were trained on the dance floor, on the people dancing, kissing, dry humping, and the pretend vampires biting skin.

Theo hadn't told Max that the real vampires had been warned away from tonight's party, offered a closed-door event with enough blood and sex to keep them sweet and their money coming in. She'd host another night, just for them, once the killer was caught and they were off the radar of a certain Detective Sergeant.

Theo must have been thinking too hard because she jerked when she felt a hand skim the top of her thigh. Max skimmed his hand from her knee to her thigh, then back again. Kaan had been right, she needed to get laid because while she wasn't a fan of too much public sex, she was ridiculously wet the harder Max caressed her skin.

She wanted his hands in other places, and she heard Kaan chuckle, glaring over at her friend for a second before she focused back on Max. He had shifted slightly, his long legs stretched out in front of him as he kept stroking her skin. Theo's skin felt like it was on fire, his touch blazing a trail that Theo had not felt in the longest time.

"What next?" she heard Max say in a low husky tone that had her looking down.

Her lips curved into a smile as she reached down to run her fingers through his hair. "Isn't this part of your plan?"

"This was definitely not part of my plan." Max muttered in a low tone, like he didn't want her to hear him, but it made her smile even more as he said a little louder. "I need my eyes on the dance floor."

Theo shifted without thinking, widening her legs. "Sit with your back to me between my legs."

Max obeyed her, and Theo couldn't stifle the question in her head if he would be so obedient in bed. He leaned against the chair, his head in line with her core but facing away. He wrapped an arm around her calf, stroking up the leather covered flesh, and this time, it was Theo who closed her eyes to hide her desire.

She could hear Kaan laughing his ass off beside her and she wanted to flip him off.

Payback would be a bitch.

Theo ran her hands over Max's shoulders, his neck, through his hair again. A handsome man who frequented the club and had spent a night or two with Kaan, came up to Simon who was standing as security and whispered in his ear, the pretend vampire looked at Kaan with open hunger. Simon made to come to Kaan to relay what was said but Kaan shook his head and drained his drink. Over the night thirty minutes of blissful agony as Max touched her, Theo watched as Kaan dismissed offer after offer and she could see her friend getting more and more pissed off.

She was about to run interference when Kannon strode up to Simon, said something and the human nodded. He was wearing tight, tight jeans, a black shirt that looked velvet to touch and Theo knew it had been a gift from Kaan to Kannon. Theo watched as Kannon shifted the collar of his shirt, then got to his knees in front of Kaan, angled his head.

Whether Kannon was doing this so that the patrons lusting after Kaan would leave him alone, or because he was sick and tired of others having what he wanted, Theo didn't know. Theo just kept her eyes on her friend in case she needed to step in, but Kaan kept his face neutral as he leaned forward in his chair, cupped one side of Kannon's neck, then lowered his mouth to his neck.

Kannon's hands gripped Kaan's thighs, enough that it would hurt.

To the vampires who had been permitted to attend tonight, it would be a display that Kannon was Kaan's, that he belonged to him. Theo noted that Kannon jerked, an erotic groan escaping his lips that was almost swallowed up by the music, and when Kaan lifted his mouth, Theo could see it was blood stained.

Kannon reached up and touched the bite marks on his neck, Kaan staring at him like he was daring Kannon to say or do something. But Kannon just smiled that mischievous smile of his, then copying Max's position, he turned and plonked down on the ground, slipping his hand under the leg of Kaan's pants and stroked the skin. Theo burst out laughing when Kaan yelled at Simon to bring him a bottle of wine, then told him to bring whiskey instead.

The night continued, and no one seemed to stand out to Theo, but she was just a vampire and Max was the hunter. Theo had skills, lots of them, but she usually knew who she was fighting and had spent too much time looking in shadows for Nyx and the twins.

Max nudged her leg with his shoulder, and she glanced down.

"I need to be out on the floor. I need to take a look at the crowd."

Theo motioned for him to back up and she got to her feet. She crooked her finger at him to bring him closer. Max did what she wanted, and Theo placed her hands on the sides of his neck. "How are you at dancing?"

"Fucking awful. Rían says I have no moves."

Theo threw back her head and laughed then said. "I'll be the judge of that. Let's hit the dance floor."

Max stood there and watched as Theo unhooked the back of her skirt and he drank up the sight of her bare skin like a man dying of thirst.

Max held out his elbow to her, and she linked his arm. Simon frowned at them as they stepped out of the VIP section, but Theo ignored him as they made their way into the crush of people. They moved to give Theo more room, wanting her, wanting Max.

Theo lifted her head to look up at Blair as the current song was winding down, and Blair gave her a mock salute, letting the music fade out, the last few bars of Zedd's song with Hayley Williams *Stay The Night* ended.

The dance floor plunged into darkness. Silence reigned. Theo could hear the panting, the moans, the grunts, and groans of pleasure, the rush of blood in the humans' veins. She could smell the sweat, the sex, the headiness of copper in the air. She was acutely aware of Max standing with her. Felt it when he put his hands on her waist.

In the darkness, Theo could pretend that she wasn't a vampire, that he wasn't her enemy. She could pretend that they were just a man and a woman on a night out, attraction lighting a fire in their veins. She placed her hands on his arms, running them up and down for a moment before Blair dropped the next track, a song by Meduza, *Upside Down* that Blair knew she liked as the lights came back on.

Theo shifted so that she was facing away from Max, her back to his. She reached behind and placed her hand on his head, then grabbed his arms and wrapped them around her middle. She let the music build up, then moved against him, felt him hard against her spine.

He might not have any natural rhythm, but he was moving with her, his hands skimming up her stomach as Theo rotated her hips, then spun to wrap her arms around his neck. She pressed her body flush to his, still moving her hips. His hands moved down to cup her ass as she ground against him, and when she dared look at him, it was like the intensity in his eyes, that hunger, sucked all the air from her lungs.

The lights went out as the song ended and Theo could stand it no longer. She grabbed Max by the front of his tee, yanking him forward and crashing her lips to his. She could almost taste his confusion, however when she nipped on his bottom lip, whatever control he thought he had fucking snapped.

His hands gripped her ass and his tongue plunged into her mouth. There was little finesse. Their teeth banged; it was sloppy. It was wild and Theo had never felt so hot in her life. His tongue plundered her mouth as his hands travelled up to cup her waist just under the curve of her breasts.

She groaned into his mouth, grinding against his erection and she wanted to take him to the fucking ground and ride him to oblivion. Max pulled his lips from hers, and when she was about to complain, he kissed his way down her jaw, to her throat and she threw back her head.

Her core clenched and she wanted his fingers, his mouth or his cock down there easing the need.

The lights came back up as Max pulled back and they stood there, both panting as Blair put another track on. Theo's blood was pounding in her ears as Max blinked, like he was coming out of some sort of spell.

His gaze snapped up, his nostrils flared, and his dark gaze scanned the area. "He's watching us."

Theo made a point of running her hands over his chest and leaned in to say. "How do you know?"

"I just do."

The killer was a vampire then. It was the only explanation for Max to have that sense that the killer was here. Or was he just focusing on any of the vampires in the room? And what did this son of Cathain feel when he was close to her?

Theo slipped her hand into his, and then Max was moving, weaving through the crowd. He must have looked fierce because people stepped out of his path, as he cut across the dance floor, back toward where Kaan was now standing with Kannon.

She glanced between the two as if looking for animosity but saw none. Well, they both wore emotionless expressions. Max gave her a gently push and she turned to see him looking over his shoulder.

"Where are you going?" Theo asked him.

"To find the killer. Stay here."

Theo didn't much care for him ordering her about like this. She might be all for it in the bedroom, but she was used to being the one giving the orders and having people obey her. She made to argue but Max was already striding out toward the crowd when someone bumped into him and he whirled round in their direction.

A young woman dressed in a leather skirt that skimmed her ass, and a leather bustier type top that showed off her tattooed arms and torso, looked at Max with a horrified expression. She took a step back in her skyscraper heels, then looked at Max and then laughed.

"What the fuck are you wearing?"

Max's arm shot out and he grabbed her and all but dragged her from the dance floor and back into the area Theo, Kaan and Kannon were standing in. Kaan made to intervene, but Theo shook her head. She needed to see how this played out.

"What the fuck are you doing here? I told you to stay the fuck at home!" Max growled, grabbing the woman's other arm, and shaking her a little. "Do you want to be a fucking victim, Shauna? You want to end up just like Megan?"

Theo could scent the fear in Max. This was the sister. Now that she was closer, Theo recognised her. Shauna glanced at Theo, then back at Max.

"I came to find her boyfriend. You weren't doing the job you're supposed to be so fucking good at. I guess you inherited our mam's kink for vampires. From the looks of the smear of lipstick on your lips."

Max blinked, absorbing the blow but he yanked his sister closer. "Go home. Go home right now or so help me God I will toss you over my shoulder and carry you out of here. If I do that Shauna and another girl dies, that's on you. I can deal with the guilt, but can you?"

Shauna shoved at him, eyes brimming with tears as she staggered back. "You're such an asshole."

"I know. So, are you leaving by yourself or am I making a scene? Your choice."

The girl looked like she wanted to argue, but then Simon stepped forward and said to Max. "I'll escort your sister out. Make sure she gets into a taxi."

Max didn't take his eyes from Shauna. He just glared her into submission. She stomped her foot and Theo had to stop herself from laughing at the childishness of it all. Shauna flipped Max off by sticking a finger in his face and then Simon was leading her out.

Max clenched his fists and pressed them to his eyes as he snarled in frustration. Theo went over and placed a hand on his arm, and he dropped his hands and looked at her.

"You good?"

"No." He ground out as he opened his eyes and scrubbed a

hand down his face. "I want to string this bastard up by his fucking spine."

"You'll get him."

Max looked out into the crowd. "It's gone now. The feeling. The killer's gone. Goddamn fucking, Shauna."

Theo glanced over her shoulder at Kannon. "Can you make sure Shauna did get in the taxi? You might charm her more than Simon."

Kannon winked and took off as Max looked out at the ground. He ran his eyes over assessing and then turned back to Theo. "He was here. He was watching. I could feel his anger. He moved like he knew this place like the back of his hand."

No normal human would be able to tell that. Max must know that the skills he had weren't just normal. What did he think about this ability of his?

His eyes landed on Theo. "You know him. He's worked for you for years. He's older than Shauna. Someone had to have noticed that he started to look at you differently. His behaviours would have changed recently."

"Changed how?" Kaan asked folding his arms across his chest.

Max frowned, his eyebrows almost meeting. "Subtle changes. Maybe he once was super compliant. Wanted to please you. Make an impression. Insert himself in your lives. Then slowly, he started to balk at taking orders. He wanted more. He wanted in on the inner circle. He resisted certain things or tasks."

Theo's head was spinning as she tried and tried to think of anyone who might have started behaving like that, but no one came to mind. In the end, it was Kaan who sucked in a breath.

Max turned his attention on Kaan and took a step toward him.

"Who? Who am I hunting?"

Kaan swallowed, then looked at Theo. "Silas said that he had started pushing back when he told him to do things. That he wanted to spend more time with you, so Silas made sure that he spent less time and kept an eye on him. He tried to get included with Mill Lane, but they turned him down. He's worked for us for years...I didn't fucking see it."

It all came rushing back to Theo. The way he'd started to touch her when she fed. The anticipation on his face that she had put down to the high a person got from feeding. Then she recalled her dismissal of him, how she had felt uncomfortable with his attention so she had taken another human to feed from.

She really was the reason for all of this, all the fucking senseless death.

Kannon came back then pushing through the crowd. "Looks like there was a struggle. I found this."

Kannon held up a black and pink sparkly phone as Max grabbed it, his expression turning to panic. "The security guard. Simon. He's the killer and he has my fucking sister."

 **MAX**

Max stared at the phone in his hand before he bolted, fear in his veins. The killer had been here. Max had riled him up by putting his hands on Theo, by kissing her, and touching her. And now the prick had his sister.

He would never forgive himself if anything happened to Shauna.

Shoving people out of his way as he rushed to the elevator, Max was aware of Theo calling his name. He didn't have time to deal with her right now. He couldn't face her knowing that part of him blamed her for not adding it all up before now. Max had been looking at her face when it had finally dawned on her that one of her heads of security was responsible for killing all her staff.

Max pressed the elevator button and then pressed the floor where he had left his clothes. Theo slipped into the elevator before the doors closed and Max growled at her. "You're not coming."

"Kaan and Kannon are getting one of my girls to hack into his personal cloud to see if he had any secret places we didn't know about. They'll call me on route to wherever we start driving too."

"They could just ring me." He snapped at her, and she just shrugged.

"Then you'd go off on your own. No matter what happens, you shouldn't have to face it alone."

The elevator stopped and Max was already stripping off his clothes before he got out of the elevator and then was yanking on his own crap. Theo surprised him by unhooking her own dress and taking it off, her boots too, before dressing in a simple pair of leggings and a t-shirt and hoodie. Then she added trainers.

Max crouched down to shove his feet into his trainers and when he straightened, Theo was ready to go. Her face was determined, and she had a little bag in her hand, but Max didn't have time to argue with her.

"Don't slow me down." Max ground out as he headed toward the elevator.

"I won't." She said, sounding like she was mildly annoyed that he suggested she might.

To be fair, Theo kept pace with him as they raced out of the club, across the road and Max unlocked his SUV. He already had the engine running as Theo got in beside him and he slammed the car into gear, peeling off of Grand Parade like a man possessed.

Theo unzipped her bag and took out a pack of wipes, wiping the makeup from her face. Then she took out her contacts before she then proceeded to start to unpin her hair as Max knew he had to tell the team what had happened.

"Call Mike." He barked out, then yanked the steering wheel as he turned left onto Washington Street as the phone rang.

"Max."

"The killer is Simon Carroll. He has Shauna."

The other man swore and Max heard him bark out a few orders before he said. "I have units on the way to his house."

Max mulled it over. If Simon was at his home and he had hurt Shauna, then Max didn't want anyone showing up before Max could return the favour.

"Give me a ten-minute head start, Mike." Max said to his boss, stealing a glance at Theo who was busy shooting off messages on her phone.

"Max..." Mike said with a sigh.

"I won't kill him." Max told him, knowing Mike would know that Max wasn't being truthful so he continued. "Not unless I have to. He has my baby sister, Mike. I played my hand, and he knows it. We are heading to his gaff now but Theo's team are looking to see if he might have a place we don't have on record."

"Legally?" Mike asked and Max glanced at Theo who was shaking her head.

"Not strictly. This is on me, Mike. This call never happened. I went rogue and went off by myself to catch the killer. The brass will believe you."

There was a pregnant pause on the other end of the line and then Mike gave a resigned sigh, and Max knew that he had won. Max hung up before Mike could change his mind and pressed his foot down harder on the accelerator.

"We'll find her."

Max gripped the steering wheel so hard it creaked, and his knuckles whitened. He didn't reply to Theo's words, just kept his eyes on the road, then he asked her. "When did you know that Simon was in love with you?"

Theo shook her head, glancing out the window. "It never dawned on me until Kaan said what he said. But Max, Simon? He's not in love with me. He's in love with the persona I put on at The Player's Lounge. Like you said, he wanted the fantasy. In reality, I'm at my happiest at home with my family, all gathered on the big ass sofa for movie or trivia nights, wearing fluffy pyjamas and eating my weight in ice-cream."

"You don't notice him watching you?"

Theo sighed, shaking her head. "I feel vapid to admit that Simon was never on my radar."

Was I?

Max wanted to ask her. He wanted...no he needed to know if she had played him.

Her phone rang, and she pressed the answer button. "Maisie, I have you on speaker. I'm with Detective Sergeant De Barra."

"Greetings Detective Hotsuff." Maisie said and Max almost laughed. "Wish we were meeting under better circumstances. Right, to business. Simon isn't home. I hacked the cameras in his apartment building, and he hasn't shown up there."

Max really wanted to know who this Maisie was and how and why Theo had a hacker working for her.

"Last month, Simon bought a black Ford transit van, and a derelict building in a housing estate in the city. I just spotted the van going through the Dunkettle on the cameras and looks like he was headed to that house."

"Good job, Maze. What's the address?" Theo asked after praising her hacker.

Maisie rattled off the address and Max braked in the middle of the road, earning a bout of horns blaring. He spun the SUV round and said to Theo, "That's the Erasmus Finn house. What the hell has this to do with Finn?"

Theo didn't answer him, just asked Maisie to keep an eye on street cams and to keep trying to track his phone. Max floored it, his heart feeling like it was about to burst out of his chest. Shauna wasn't like him. Simon would hurt her, and it would take a little bit of her when he did.

It had been Max's oath to her on the night Aideen had killed Elliot that had been the driving force of all his actions to this point, the promise he had kept to himself since that day. The one his dad had asked him not too long before he died, to always look after his sister, no matter what happened to him or his mam.

And on the night their lives were changed forever, Max finally understood why his dad had asked it of him.

The Detective questioning him about what had happened led Max out of the kitchen and into the living room. The Detective motioned for him to take a seat, but Max had blood on his clothes, and his face, and he didn't want to get blood on the white couch. There would be a funeral, and people would probably call to the house. They'd have to come sit in the good room.

"I want to see my sister." Max told the detective, who shook his head.

"Not yet, kid. We gotta go over this for a while yet."

Max folded his arms across his chest. "I'm not telling you another fucking thing until my lawyer is present and I see my sister. I'm still classed as a minor, so you can't speak to me without an adult present. So, I'm going to see my sister and your questions can wait."

Max bolted out of the room and up the stairs as the Detective yelled at him to hang on. He could hear Shauna crying in her room, trying to be coaxed by a female voice and Max barged into the room and ordered everyone out.

He wrapped his arms around Shauna. "Hey, it's okay. I've got you. I won't let anyone hurt you."

Shauna wrapped her own arms around his waist and Max let her cry, unable to cry himself. Seeing his mam kill his dad had seemed to flip a switch inside him and it was like his emotions had just turned off.

Lifting her head, Shauna looked at Max as tears still slipped down her cheeks. "Did mam really kill dad?"

"Ya, she did."

"What happens to us now? Will I go into care?"

Max shook his head vigorously. "Hell no. I'll fix it. I'll sort everything out. I've got you and I always will."

His sister looked at him with utter belief and his stomach clenched. He could do this right? He could keep her safe from what came next even if it meant she grew to hate him a little bit. That was his job now. To protect her from the fallout.

"It was my job to keep her safe. I promised my dad that I would."

"We'll get her back. We have to trust that we will."

Max kept his eyes on the road as he told Theo. "I told Mike I wouldn't kill him. I lied. If he harmed even a single hair on Shauna's head, if I see one mark or bruise on her face then he's dead, Theo. If you can't deal with that, I can let you out the car and Kaan can come get you."

He felt Theo looking at him as she replied softly. "Sometimes, killing a person is justifiable. The creatures of this world who inflict pain. Who steal innocence. Who use their power over the waste to make themselves feel superior. Death is sometimes far too quick for them."

Her answer surprised him, and he stole a quick glance at her. "Should I ask the obvious questions or am I better off not knowing?"

Theo waved a hand in the air. "I believe it's called plausible deniability, and I will deny we ever had this conversation."

Max drove onto the street that he had driven down once before, and they both spotted the van at the same time. Slamming on the breaks, Max was out of the car, having grabbed his gun from the glove box and making sure it was loaded.

Theo had hopped out after him, and Max turned to look at her. "If I asked you nicely to stay in the SUV, would you?"

"No. And if you try and force me, I'll just get out and follow you anyways."

Max didn't have time to argue with Theo, so he just told her to stay behind him, and stay close and alert. He felt a wave of pain in his gut, not as strong as it had been when he'd come to this house before, but it was there, like a bad omen.

Creeping up to the front door, Max held up his gun, and used his free hand to try the door. It opened easily but squealed when he pushed it open, no doubt alerting Simon that they had arrived. Max stepped over the threshold, the scent of mould and damp tickling his nostrils. The boarded-up windows made it even darker in the house and Max's eyes darted around as he remembered the last time he'd been here.

Max felt like the pain was going to cripple him if he didn't do what his head was screaming at him to do. He felt like a dumb fuck as he got out of his car and walked up the path, then rang the doorbell.

Heavy footsteps sounded before the door opened and a man stood there glaring at him.

And Max knew with utmost certainly that this was the man who he'd been hunting.

The man was almost seven foot tall with hair that was alabaster in colour. His eyes were a murky sort of brown and he smelled of sweat and blood.

Max flashed the man a charming smile, knowing he needed to get his foot inside that door. "Hey man, my car got a flat tyre and my phone fucking died on me. Any chance I can call my breakdown assist?"

"Sure. No hassle."

The man let Max in and immediately Max took in the scene. His gaze landed on the sofa in full view of the hall and Max's heart sank. He spotted the pink bunny that was taken with the most recent kidnap victim girl. It was nestled in with other toys, and bears, one for each of his kills. The bastard had kept trophies.

Max looked back at the man and the monster realized that Max knew who he was. He lunged for Max, snarling, faster and stronger than anyone Max had fought against before. Max cocked out his leg, tripping him and when the bigger man stumbled, Max shoved him hard.

Max watched as the man went backwards, the coat hanger on the wall going right into him. It slid through his skin like a knife through butter, right in the centre of his chest.

Max stared at the flailing man, blood pouring from the wound and somehow, Max knew that the asshole would survive it. He could be free to hurt more children. Reaching down, he withdrew the hunting knife from the sheath at his ankle, and listened as the blood in his veins sang. He didn't know when he did it, but between one blink and the next, Max had plunged the blade into the man's heart, and he stopped moving.

Max pulled the knife out of the dead man's chest and this over-whelming sense of rightness flooded his veins, making him light-headed. He'd never killed a man before.

Still holding the knife, Max took out his phone and called his boss, Mike O'Connor.

When Mike answered, Max just said. "I found the killer. I killed him. I need to go find the girl. You should come."

Mike had been shouting at him as he'd rattled off the address, hung up and went in search of the kidnapped girl.

"Max?"

The sound of Theo's voice dragged him from his memories. She placed a hand on the small of his back and urged him forward. Max followed his instincts, this phantom knowledge that the man they'd been hunting was in this house, breathing the same air as he was. His muscles tightened, and even though his heart had been racing not thirty seconds ago, it had now returned to a normal rhythm.

He was stupidly calm for a man who was absolutely certain he was about to come face to face with a monster so vile, that

Max knew he could no longer be called human. That a monster was holding his sister's life in his hands.

He had seen what Simon had done to his victims and as a man who had already seen a member of his family bleeding on the ground, he wasn't in a hurry to see another person he cared about brutalized.

The floorboards under Max creaked as he made his way down the hallway. He felt a kiss of cold air sweep under his pant leg, and he looked at the wall next to him. He stared at it, then put his free hand on the wall and pushed, hard.

Max heard a click, and the wall slid open. He knew that this secret basement had been where Erasmus Finn had kept his kidnapped victims, where he killed them. Theo's hand was still on the small of his back as he started to head down the stairs.

He thought he heard a slight whimper as he cocked his gun and continued downward, his eyes adjusting to the dim overhead lights. The basement appeared empty as his feet touched the concrete. He surveyed the room, heard a grunt and Max spun to point his gun in the direction of the noise.

His eyes landed on Shauna. She was unconscious, blood on her forehead and face. She was slumped next to a wooden beam, her hands and legs bound by a rope. Max wanted to rush forward to her and shake her, to make sure she was alive, but he needed to find Simon Caroll and make him pay for what he had done.

Max could sense that Simon was here with them in the basement, but he couldn't pinpoint where exactly. It was like whatever sense he had was diluted. Yet he could feel Theo's presence behind him.

"Come on out, Caroll. Give yourself up. It's over now."

Max heard a bitter laugh and spun toward the sound.

"It's not over, Detective Sergeant. For you it's only beginning."

Max heard the lick of truth in his words, but Max had no clue as to what he was referring to. Looking at Theo, Max held up his finger to his lips, and pushed Theo to the space under the stairs as he, moved into the centre of the basement.

"C'mon, Simon. Let's have a chat, you, and me. Tell me all about it and I'll see if I can help you. I'll put the gun away."

Simon laughed. "We both know if I show myself, then I'm not leaving this basement alive. I'm dead either way. But I think it's time you knew the truth, Max De Barra. About who you are. About what you are."

Adrenaline shot through his veins. Yes, he heard his blood sing. This is what you have to know. Max was about to ask Simon, to get the answers that he obviously needed. He took a step further into the dark of the basement, then a moment too late, he heard the movement of feet a split second before something whacked him in the back of the head. Pain splintered through his skull and Max staggered, before he crumpled to the ground, his vision swimming. Max heard his gun clatter to the floor, and as he tried to force himself to get back up again, but darkness came to claim him.

THEO

Guilt threatened to undo her as Theo looked down at Max's unconscious form. She hadn't wanted to hurt him, but if Simon knew what he was, if they had been too blasé about keeping this from getting out and let Simon overhear them, then it was up to Theo to fix the issue.

There was no way that Max deserved to be thrown into their world like this.

Simon stepped out into view and clapped his hands. "Nice shot."

Theo braced her feet slightly apart and shrugged. "I've had some practice. It's just you and me now, Simon. Isn't that what you wanted?"

Simon laughed, shaking his head. "I'd have preferred you on your knees. Or face down, ass in the air."

Theo rolled her eyes. "I mean, that's so fucking romantic how could a vampire refuse?"

Simon's face contorted in rage, and his hands balled into fists. "You think you are so much better than me. You, Kaan, the rest of your Scion. But if it wasn't for humans like me, you wouldn't survive."

While he was distracted, Theo passed the plank of wood from hand to hand and then she gave Simon a massive smile. "Simon, catch."

She threw the plank of wood at Simon, and he barely caught it, then let it fall to the floor right beside Max who was still out cold. He looked at the wood, then lifted his gaze to Theo.

"What the fuck was that about?" Simon demanded.

"You attacked a guard. Now your prints are on the wood."

Simon sneered at Theo. "What about your prints?"

Theo flashed her fangs. "My prints got on it when I bashed your brains out on the basement floor. Very Lady Macbeth of me but whatever."

Simon gave her a look that was a cross between lust and fear. Theo wanted to claw out his carotid with her bare fucking hands and let him fucking bleed out on this goddam floor. She wanted to rip his spine from his body and beat him to death with it. How the fuck had she been this oblivious?

Simon was never on my radar.

That was the truth of it. Simon had never been on her radar. She fed from him, yes, like she had many humans in her lifetime but ever since Nyx had started to kill those close to her, her Zayan, her lovers, her food, Theo had been very careful not to form attachments. The only reason the last feeding with Simon had gone to more than just feeding, where she had allowed the ghost of a touch, was because she had been thinking about Max.

Theo needed to know more about why he did what he did. She needed to probe him for answers before Max woke up. She'd have to try and kill him before then, for her story to work.

"Why try and get my attention this way? What did you hope to achieve?"

Simon paced back and forth, keeping his eyes on Theo. "I served you all for over a decade. I watched you fuck and feed and never age a bloody day. Ye had women and men worshipping at your feet. I was good at my job and you still looked after the whores better than me."

Theo folded her arms across her chest but refrained from saying anything. She just let him get his secrets off his chest.

"They let me watch yano? They knew I wanted to join in, and they let me watch. Camile got off knowing that I wanted in on their poly group. Then she used to invite me to watch her when she let the vampires fuck her, feed from her. When I asked to join, they all laughed and told me that I wasn't man enough."

Theo swallowed hard. "So, you showed them."

Simon smiled and his eyes were emotionless as he looked at Theo. "I did. For embarrassing me I made Camile fuck herself with the leg of the chair. I enjoyed watching them while they were all terrified."

"Okay," Theo replied, shifting her weight slightly, getting herself ready to launch herself forward if she needed to. "I understand that. I do. But what about Molly? What about Mike? And Fallon? Tell me about them."

Simon threw back his head and laughed. "Molly. You dressed her up to look like you. God, I used to imagine what it would be like to have you both. I wanted you to know that she was killed for pretending to be you. A poor substitute. And Mike, fucking dumbass came to me and told me that I was acting weird and that he was gonna report me to Silas."

That was what they suspected but now at least it was confirmed.

"I went to his house with a slab of beer as a peace offering and killed him. It got easier the more I did it. They told me it would."

They told me it would.

Simon had someone egging him on.

"Fallon got drunk one night and I drove her home. She kissed me and we were gonna have sex but I couldn't ..."

Theo bit the inside of her mouth not to laugh. This totally wasn't the time to be laughing because Simon, when given the chance to have sex with one of the most beautiful women in Cork, couldn't get it up.

"She laughed at me, told me to get out and she would finish herself off. I killed her and the moment she started bleeding, I was rock hard. I fucked her then, as she bled out. Wore a condom so no DNA."

Simon seemed almost proud of the fact he had engaged in safe sex while the woman he was inside was dying. He was looking at Theo like he was expecting her to applaud his methods, like he needed her approval.

Theo opened her mouth to try and get more information from Simon, but it would seem, the killer was feeling very chatty tonight.

"Erasmus was going to make me a vampire. He promised and then he fucking died. I went and fetched all those kids for him and then the fucker died before he could turn me. He'd fed me his blood, yano, with every kid I brought him, he fed me."

If Theo hadn't already been certain she was gonna kill this bastard, she sure as shit was gonna do it now. They had never ever suspected that Finn had an accomplice. And this also made sense as to why Max could feel Simon but not as much as a full vampire. Max was sensing the vampire blood in Simon's veins.

But Erasmus Finn had been dead nearly three years. The vampire blood left from Finn would be minute now if any at all. That meant that Simon had another vampire guiding his hand.

"I asked Kaan to make me a vampire after Finn died. He chuckled and told me that would never happen because you needed me as human security. I asked him if it was because he didn't find me attractive, because I would blow him if that's what it took to be a vampire, and he just walked away."

Kaan had never told her that. Fuck...if he'd told her then Theo would have probably fired him. No, she knew that Simon would already be maggots and bones in the dirt by now. She's have killed him for it. Those who craved immortality usually ended up being the ones who didn't take well to it. Simon would have found a way to do it eventually.

"I couldn't ask you because everyone knows you don't make any Zayan. I ran out of blood. Finn had given me some spares in case we couldn't see each other for a while, and I couldn't find any other vampire who would give me their blood without your permission."

Theo was sure that if Simon looked hard enough, in the murkier parts of the city, he would have found a vampire to let him drink their blood. They were all lucky that he'd never found them.

"It hurt not to drink the blood. I tried human blood, and it just didn't hit the same. Then he found me in a brothel trying to convince a vampire to let me feed. He made me an offer, I couldn't refuse."

Theo's stomach clenched. Nyx liked to frequent brothels. Emery was proof of that, but Theo knew if Nyx had been behind all of this, then he would have just told her. He never lied to her about anything like that because it was more fun for him to let her know. He wanted her to suffer. He would have told her all the sordid details so that she absorbed the blame and then he'd taken pleasure in her pain.

Could he have changed tactics?

"I can see you trying to figure it all out in your head, Theo. My benefactor gave me all the little details. The Greek quote, the Romanian one, he told me all about your past. He knew that you were only scared of one Velesan so we framed it to look like it was the Lord of Night and his terror twins."

For one sliver of a moment, Theo wondered if she had a traitor in her Scion. She pondered the blow it would be to find out that she had someone in her inner circle who had betrayed her. Her mind was jumbled with thoughts and reasons as to why someone would side with a human to get to her.

Simon laughed, taking glee in her silence. "I thought Erasmus had potent blood, but this vampire, man, it was like being drunk and high all at once." Simon took a step toward Theo, and she didn't so much as blink. "What would your blood taste like? I know you have power. One taste. Just one taste, Theo."

"I'd snap your neck before you even got near me, Simon."

Her voice was cold, clinical, and yet, Simon only smiled. "A man can dream, right? When he comes to take over your Scion, he'll give you to me when he's done with you. For too long, vampires have hidden themselves from the world. Vampires were born to rule. They need to rule."

This broke down rhetoric was sounding awfully familiar to Theo.

"The old ways need to be reinstated." Simon told her in a matter-of-fact tone. "Once he become Suzerain of the Scion, things will change. The Order of the Dragon will be reinstated. The making of impure vampires will be sanctioned, with quotas per annum. Humans will bow down to the king of all vampires, or they will die."

Simon lifted his gaze to hers. "In order for the vampire race to be treated like Gods again, a child needed to be born to re-establish the bloodline. You have been chosen to be mother and queen of the new true blood vampire race."

Theo burst out laughing. She couldn't help herself.

She must have startled Simon because he jerked backwards and as she tried to stop laughing, and hiccupped, Simon's face contorted into an angry scowl.

"Stop fucking laughing!" Simon screamed at Theo, and she put a hand on her chest to try and regain her composure.

"Oh my God, Henry...Henry and his damn fucking twisted head is behind all this? Why the fuck would he think that I would even entertain the idea of having a child with him? He's been sprouting this bullshit since the day I met him."

Now that Theo had her answers, she needed to get rid of Simon and quickly before Max woke up. The knock she'd given him to the head wasn't too hard, well, not for a Cathainite so given another while, he should be up and that wouldn't do.

Theo snarled, thinking it was time to show Simon exactly what a vampire was. "You simpleton. You fool. Henry used you. He's over in his homeland with his harem, in the place he thinks of as his castle. He can deny it all. Tell us you made it all up and because his hands didn't fucking touch anything, and I can do fuck all to him without proof."

Simon retreated a step as Theo let her eyes bleed to red. She elongated her fangs, felt her gums shift to let them down fully. Her face shifted a little and she let Simon see the full monsters' vampires could be. Theo inhaled and she could scent his fear.

Good. Simon should be afraid.

"Did Henry tell you that I abhor rapists and child molesters? Did he tell you of the scores of vampires I hunted down and killed for even daring to think of such a heinous act? Did he tell you of the rapist in my hometown whose dick I chopped off and put on a spike in a village he terrorised? I guess I inherited some family traits after all."

Simon scrambled to pick up the plank of wood and swung it at Theo. She grabbed the end of the plank and yanked hard, pulling Simon closer to her. He let go as he stumbled, and then Theo swept his legs out from underneath him with the plank.

He landed on his back and Theo dropped the plank, leaping forward and straddling Simon's waist. He tried to struggle, but Theo clamped her thighs tight and put her hand on his chest, just over his heart, the organ pounding against Simon's chest as if it knew that Simon was looking at his death.

Theo put a little pressure, knowing that she could kill him with her bare hands, crush his chest and pierce his heart. She didn't have long enough to take her time. Theo knew that but Simon didn't.

"I should do to you what you did to your victims. I should cut you, make you bleed. Taste your fear and enjoy it. I should take that plank of wood and shove it so far up your ass that you get splinters in your mouth. I should humiliate you and leave you like that for someone to find."

Simon whimpered. "Please Theo. I only wanted you to see me."

Theo pressed down on Simon's chest as she snarled. "I see you now, Simon. I fucking see you."

Theo heard a moan over her shoulder, and she swore, knowing she was out of time. She took a breath and her face returned to normal, gone was any trace that she was a vampire. She angled her head and leaned invto whisper in Simon's ear. "You got off lucky. I hope you rot in hell."

Simon had a look of confusion on his face and then Theo rolled them over, placing her under Simon so that he was straddling her. She reached between them and ripped her hoodie and started to cry.

"No, please, Simon. Don't hurt me."

She screamed and Simon recoiled, straightening his back. Theo heard the gun go off and Simon's body jerked once, twice before falling toward her. Theo almost rolled her eyes as she let out a damsel in distress cry and then Simon's body was pulled off her.

Max crouched down in front of her, his face bloody, his lips too, as he reached out, helped her sit up and cupped her cheek. "Did he hurt you?"

She offered him a grateful smile. "No. You stopped him. Thank you."

Max was looking at her with suspicion in his eyes, so Theo leaned forward and pressed a kiss to his lips. She tasted his blood and she wanted to crawl into his lap and sink her fangs into his neck and drink her fill of him. There was power, untamed, and wild in his veins.

This was bad. This was so fucking bad.

She broke the kiss, her chest heaving as Max got to his feet, swayed a little, then just watched her as she scrambled to her feet. She pulled her torn hoodie around her, as Max pulled out his phone and called his boss to tell them where they were. When he had hung up, he asked her about what Simon had said to her while he was out, but Theo distracted him by telling him to go look at his sister.

Max went over to Shauna, checked her pulse and the relief on his face was contagious. Theo shouldn't be this invested in Max and his family, but she was dammit. She needed to put some distance between them. The case was over, and they had no need to see each other again. Right?

Max's sister stirred and then her eyes darted open and she was about to scream when Max brushed her hair off her face. "Hey, it's me. I got you. I've always got you."

Shauna threw her arms around Max's neck, sobbing as the wail of sirens came closer and then she heard Max's boss Mike shout for him. The Gardaí came down the stairs, Mike leading the charge. He took one look at the scene then at Max, as if he had known Max would kill him.

"He tried to rape me when Max was unconscious. Max shot Simon to save me." Theo said, and the other man's eyes softened.

"Are you okay, Ms. Caden?"

Theo nodded, playing her part of defenceless female. "I am now. Thanks to Max."

Mike reached out and gave her shoulder a squeeze, before heading over to Max who was arguing with the paramedics who wanted to take Shauna and himself to the hospital. Mike managed to talk him round, the paramedics took Shauna from the room as Mike turned to Max and Theo, glancing at Simon for a moment before he asked them what the hell had just happened. Max looked at Theo, then back at Mike, as Theo pulled out her phone and texted Kaan to come get her at Erasmus Finn's house.

The Scion would meet to discuss Henry's motives. To make a decision on how next to proceed. And she was sure that they would discuss the situation they now faced with Max. He was a threat to the safety of the Scion, far greater than Henry and his madness. Theo had to protect her family.

Even if it meant killing the man who had ignited a flame inside her for the first time in centuries.

Life was a fucking bitch, wasn't it?

MAX

Max's head was killing him as Mike glared at him and Theo, demanding they tell him what happened. He wanted to find out from Theo what had happened when he'd been knocked out, and then go check on Shauna at the hospital. His lips still burned from the kiss Theo had given him, but why the hell did it feel like she'd been trying to distract him?

Ríán came down the stairs, took one look at the three of them lingering in the basement, and after asking Max if everyone was okay, ordered them away from the body. Theo went up the stairs first, Mike in between them, and when Max asked Mike to give him and Theo a minute, Mike shook his head.

"Can't lad. We can't have it looking like you two were sorting out your stories to make sure they were the same. You can talk to her after I've taken both your statements. So do as you're told for once and shut up and listen to me."

Mike then ordered him to the back of an ambulance to get his head checked out, and when Max complained, Mike steered Theo toward the ambulances. Max sat on the back of the ambulance while a paramedic looked at the gash on his head, and he listened to every word Theo was saying.

"After he hit Max, he told me he loved me. That he was mad at me for not noticing him. He thought I'd be more attracted to him if he acted the part of a vampire lover. Then he saw me and Max at the club and he was so angry that he wanted to punish Max. That was why he took Shauna. He took Megan to distract Max, to warn him off."

Theo sniffled, and Mike gave her a pack of tissues. She dabbed at her eyes before continuing, but there was this feeling in the pit of Max's stomach that all he was hearing was lies. He hoped it was just the concussion making him feel sick.

"I tried to talk him into giving himself up. But he tried to kiss me, and I pushed him away. That was when he...that was when."

She looked away then, like she couldn't say the words, and Mike reached out and took her hand.

"It's okay, Ms. Caden. You're safe now."

Max almost rolled his eyes, but he thought it would hurt too much.

The paramedic treating Max told Mike he had a severe laceration to the back of his head and another cut from when his head had bounced off the floor. She recommended Max go to hospital for stitches. Max shook his head and told the paramedic to just put some glue on the wound and he'd be grand. When she had looked horrified at Max, he'd gone into the ambulance himself and gotten the glue.

It was only when the paramedic realized that he actually intended to try and glue the wound himself did she reluctantly do it herself. Mike quizzed him on what happened, and Max told him that Simon had caught him off guard, knocking him unconscious and when he woke, Simon was on top of Theo.

"I discharged my weapon twice, then shoved his body off Theo. After checking that she was okay, I called you and then went to check on Shauna. You lot got here pretty quickly."

Mike snorted. "I got an anonymous text from an untraceable number telling us where you were." He glanced at Theo. "This got anything to do with your little hacker?"

Theo gave Mike a coy smile. "What hacker, Superintendent?"

Mike rolled his eyes and then looked between Max and Theo. "I'll give you two a moment."

Leaving them alone, Max waved off the paramedic and got to his feet. He felt steadier now, and the pain in his head was slowly dissipating. Theo rubbed her arms and was looking toward the house instead of looking at him.

"What really happened?" Max ground out and Theo snapped her head in his direction.

"I'm sorry, what?"

"You heard me. What the fuck happened when I was knocked out?"

Theo's gaze narrowed as she glared at him. "Max, you saw it with your own eyes. Do you really think I'd lie about something like this?"

Max arched his brows as if to say, absofuckinglutely, and Theo threw her hands up in the air.

"Unfuckingbelievable."

She made to storm off and Max snapped out his hand to grab her arm. She spun around, a vicious look on her face like she wanted to deck him. But when she opened her mouth an eerily calm voice said. "Take your hand off me, Detective Sergeant."

Max hesitated for half a heartbeat before he removed his hand. "Why this house? Why this fucking hellhole of a house?"

Theo shrugged, a pissed off expression on her face. "I don't know, Max. Maybe he was a fanboy. Maybe Simon had done his research and knew this house might rattle you. Who the fuck knows what he was thinking. But it's over now and he's dead. I guess we're done."

Somehow, it didn't sound like Theo was talking about the murder hunt.

Max was about to ask her what she meant when he heard the rumble of an engine nearby and then Kaan Sydin was striding right on through the police cordon and heading straight for Theo, and Max knew the moment was gone.

Theo rushed to Kaan, wrapped her arms around his waist and he kissed the top of her head. Max felt like he wanted to rip Theo from his arms, and it must have shown on his face because Kaan arched his brows in clear amusement.

"I assume you are done with Theo tonight, gentlemen?"

Max was about to argue, when Mike appeared. "Ms. Caden is free to go. If we have any more questions, then we know where to find her."

Kaan reached inside the pocket of his jacket, then after untangling Theo from him, he strode over and handed Mike a business card. "I forgot to mention before, but I am Ms. Caden's lawyer and I would ask that you please contact me should you wish to arrange an appointment to speak to her."

He gave Max a very smug grin before he turned back to Theo and asked her if she was ready to go. Theo glanced at Max, a little flash of something in her eyes before she looked back at Kaan and nodded.

Max wasn't about to let her walk away without letting her know he wasn't going anywhere anytime soon. Mike nudged his elbow as he called her name, Theo turning to look right at him, those haunting green eyes holding his.

"I'll see you around, Ms. Caden."

Theo's lips curved into a tight smile. "I'm sure you will, Detective Sergeant De Barra. I'm sure you will."

And then she was gone, and Max felt like the air had been sucked from his lungs.

"You believe any of the bullshit story she told us?" Mike said in a low tone to Max, and Max was impressed at how well Mike had been able to placate Theo.

"Not in the fucking slightest." Max told his boss and Mike nodded.

"Good. Not everything adds up, Lad. It's too fucking neat and tidy."

Max had to agree with him on that. There was something more going on at The Player's Lounge and with Theo Caden, and it was an itch Max would need to scratch or it might drive him mad.

"Let's get you to the hospital to see your sister and then we can talk."

Mike took Max's keys and drove his SUV to the hospital. They didn't speak until Mike had parked the car in the hospital car park, and then he began, his eyes looking out into the night.

"What kind of nightclub owner has a hacker on staff?"

"You thinking organised crime?" Max asked, clicking off his seatbelt.

"Maybe," Mike said, then added. "But even that doesn't feel right. We need to tread carefully on this, Max. If they think we are still looking into them, that we haven't bought their bullshit, then they will close ranks. The last couple weeks, I've had the team looking for someone that we might be able to turn informant. That entire staff must be loyal as fuck or scared shitless because we couldn't narrow down even a potential. We need someone on the inside."

Max shook his head, scrubbing a hand down his face. "Something tells me that getting someone inside would be damn near impossible. They even had cameras in their employee's home. As you said, a hacker on retainer. We might have to look at other avenues. Think outside the box."

"But we keep digging. This is our city, Max. Our goddamn city."

Max agreed with Mike, and when a patrol car parked beside Max's SUV, Mike inclined his head. "Go see your sister. We can talk in a day or two. I'll make sure internal affairs clear ya, and then, we can get stuck in. I see the way you looked at her, lad. Can you put aside your attraction and get stuck in? Sure, look who I'm talking to. Master at setting aside your emotions, you are."

Max huffed out a laugh, getting out of his car and headed toward the emergency department. A nurse took one look at him and tried to ask him where he was bleeding from. She didn't seem to believe him that someone had already glued his head and he was grand. He went to the bathroom and washed the blood from his face, leaving his hair alone since that would sting like a bitch when he did wash it.

His phone rang, and he saw it was Rían. Max sighed, then answered it. "I'm fine."

"Sure ya are. Have you seen Shauna yet?"

"Just on my way to her now. Apparently walking into a hospital with your face caked in blood isn't the brightest idea."

Rían laughed down the phone. "I need to go autopsy the killer's body. You need me to stop off at your gaff and check on JD?"

"Ya, please. Let me know if you find anything weird on the body."

Rían was silent for a moment. "Define weird?"

"Well, if the fucker had any other wounds not from the two bullets I put in him, that's weird."

"I'd tell you that you are cranky when you get hit over the head but you're always fucking cranky. I'm surprised the wood didn't snap in half when it came into contact with your hard head."

Rían hung up on him before Max could retort, but the banter with his friend had eased some of the tension in him. He took a piss and finished cleaning up, then went to see his sister.

Max asked the nurse at the desk where his sister was, flashing his badge before she told him she was in the third bay. He strode in, pulled back the curtain and stepped inside. Shauna looked like she was sleeping. She had a bandage on her forehead, and one wrapped around her wrist.

Max wished Simon Carroll was still alive so he could put a few more bullets in him.

Shauna opened her eyes, and they widened when she saw him. "You came."

He must have looked confused because Shauna chewed her bottom lip, then sat up a little in the bed. "I thought you would put the job before me. I texted Rían to come, but he's like you too. The job comes first."

Max took one of the plastic chairs and dragged it over to sit down next to Shauna's bed. "Of course I came. You're the only family I have, Shauna. Besides, my work is done. That asshole is dead and there's nothing more for me to do."

He gave her a smile and Shauna rolled her eyes.

"You wanna tell me what happened? What did he say to you?"

"Are you asking as my brother or as a Detective?" Shauna asked him snarkily.

Max shrugged, resting his elbows on his knees and his face in his hands. "Both. I know you probably think that's a fucking bullshit answer, but I am who I am, Shauna. You gotta learn to accept that about me."

Shauna reached out and took a drink of water, not commenting on what Max had said, but then she told him a little about what happened. "I was cursing you leaving the club. Then the guy, Simon, he told me that he was sorry and it wasn't personal, but you had to be taught a lesson."

Anger bubbled in his veins. It was true, Shauna had been hurt because of him.

"The woman you were with, that's Theo Caden, right? She owns The Player's Lounge, right?"

Max nodded, and Shauna carried on. "He was rambling about her, under his breath. I couldn't hear him too well from the back of the van, but he was pissed at her. Said something about you and her making out in the middle of the dance floor even after all he had done for her. He was afraid of someone as well...said he wouldn't be happy."

Simon Caroll had an accomplice.

Fuck...this wasn't over at all, was it?

Shauna looked shattered then, and Max didn't push her for anymore information. Turned out that Shauna had a bruised wrist and that cut on her head from when Simon hit her with something to knock her out. She'd passed the concussion proto-col, so Max was free to take her home.

He'd stopped on the way home and bought her an ice cream cone. It might be stupid o'clock in the morning but when she laughed at him eating his own 99, Max knew he'd made the right choice. They picked up some Chinese food, then went home.

Shauna went to her room to shower and change, and Max did the same. His head did sting when he washed his hair, and yet, not as much as he had expected. When he touched his fingers to the back of his head, he was surprised that it wasn't as bad as he was expecting.

Paramedic had done an excellent job with that glue.

Max threw on a pair of loose joggers, a t-shirt, and a plain black hoodie and went downstairs to see Shauna waiting on the couch, JD's head in her lap as she pointed to the plate on the table in front of her.

"I heated yours up. Don't think I'll sleep much. You wanna watch some mindless TV with me?"

Max gave his sister a grin and plonked himself down on the

couch beside her. "No bloody Love Island or Married at First Sight. I'd like to enjoy my food."

Shauna laughed, then sobered a little. "I used to joke with Megan that I was gonna sign you up for a show like that. She told me I was insane because the fact that you were sitting on millions would make great TV and we should try and get The Batchelor on board."

Max rolled his eyes and reached over and stole a prawn cracker. "You have more of a shot with Rían. I think the producers would take one look at my face and realize I have the perfect face to be on the radio."

Shauna frowned at him. "You don't look that much like a troll, Max."

"That is the nicest thing you've ever said to me."

"Ya, well don't get used to it. I have to be nice to you for a while since you came to my rescue."

Max was laughing as Shauna scrolled through the recordings on the TV and then threw on The Great British Bake Off. He wanted to tell her to turn the shite off, but Max just sat there and ate his Chinese food, and just let himself enjoy the fact for the first time in years, his sister was willingly spending time with him.

A few episodes in, Shauna yawned, setting her plate on the coffee table, and she stroked JD's head. She scooted closer to Max, then rested her head on his shoulder. Max reached behind them and grabbed the blanket, getting JD to lift his head so Max could drape the blanket over her.

"What happens now?" She asked softly.

Max let out a sigh, then answered her. "You grieve the friend you lost. You do that and then you move on. The bastard doesn't get to have you as another victim, Shauna. You go on with your life because Megan would want you to. Some days you'll forget and that will bring it all back to you. Or you'll laugh at something and think, I must tell Megan that, and you won't be able to. Life is short, Shauna. Live it. And mean it."

"Is that what you did, after dad?" She asked and Max wasn't sure how to answer her.

"After dad, I had you to look out for. I knew I was your big brother and I had to protect you from it all. Even if that meant you hated me. And I do what I can to make sure that families who had loved ones killed, get their own closure."

Shauna sat up and looked at him. "I never hated you, Max. I hated her. And I felt like you chose her over dad. Over me."

Max shook his head, made to answer her when his phone rang. He pulled it out of his pocket, surprised to see the name of the residential care home Aideen was in calling. Max lifted his eyes to Shauna, and he knew instantly that the moment had been shattered.

"Don't answer. For one fucking night after what we've been through, choose me over her."

Max was torn, unsure of what to do but Shauna grabbed his phone and disconnected the call. It immediately rang again after a couple of seconds. He tapped Shauna's hand and took the phone from her.

"Shauna, she might be ill. I have to answer."

"Go on then, choose her again. I hope the fucking bitch finally did the world a favour and just died!"

He half expected Shauna to storm from the room, but she stayed firm in her seat, her arms folded across her chest. The phone stopped ringing, but then started again, and Max slide his finger on the screen to answer the phone.

"Max De Barra."

"Max, it is Adisa. You must come quickly."

"What happened?" Max asked her, getting to his feet.

"Your mother went crazy. She got out of her room and killed a nurse. She said he was a vampire. You must come quickly. We are in lockdown...your mother is still hunting vampires."

The Murdering Hour Tolls Again In
"Dwell In Darkness"

PLAYLISTS

Listen to the Own the Night Playlist on Spotify

SCAN ME

ACKNOWLEDGMENTS

None of this would be possible without an amazing team supporting me! Many thanks to:

Publishing House: CTP Publishing
Cover design: Gem Promotions
Interior Formating: Gem Promotions
Proof Reading: Ashley Brilinski

∼

And as always:
Thank you to all the readers!
Whether this is your first book by me or you've been with me for years! I only get to do this because of you, and I am eternally grateful to each and every one of you who took a chance on this Irish author.

ALSO BY SUSAN HARRIS

DEFY THE STARS

A Tale of Two Houses, book 1
Until Death Do Us Part, book 2
In Defiance of the Stars, book 3
Courting Darkness, a novella

THE EVER CHACE CHRONICLES

Skin & Bones, book 1
Collateral Damage, book 2
Smoke & Mirrors, book 3
Night of the Hunter, book 4
Never Back Down, book 5
Shortcut to the Grave, book 6
Arsonist's Lullaby, book 7
Of Gods And Monsters, book 8

THE SANGUINE CROWN

Chaos Theory, book 1
Butterfly Effect, book 2
Wicked Game, book 3
Burn Notice, book 4
Fight Song, book 5

OTHER BOOKS

Shattered Memories - A Standalone Novel

∼

A Lot Like Christmas - Anthology

The Rebel County Universe which will span eight different businesses, all intersecting with characters popping up when you least expect them.

~

The Rebel Racers Trilogy
Available Now:
Adrenaline Junkie (Rebel Racers Book 1)
All or Nothing (Rebel Racers Book 2)
Crash and Burn (Rebel Racers Book 3)

The Rebel Rock Trilogy
Available Now:
Centre Stage (Rebel Rock Book 1)
Strings Attached (Rebel Rock Book 2)
Make or Break (Rebel Rock Book 3)

The Rebel Ink Trilogy
Available Now:
Breaking the Habit (Rebel Ink Book 1)
Uncomfortably Numb (Rebel Ink Book 2)
Secrets In Ink (Rebel Ink Book 3)

The Rebel Books Trilogy
Available Now:
Best Laid Plans (Rebel Books Book 1)
More Than Words (Rebel Books Book 2)
Take the Lead (Rebel Books Book 3)

Coming Soon:
The Rebel PR Trilogy
The Rebel Rescue Trilogy

ABOUT THE AUTHOR

Susan Harris is a writer from Cork, Ireland and when she's not torturing her readers with heart-wrenching plot twists or killer cliffhangers, she's probably getting some new book related ink, binging her latest TV or music obsession, or with her nose in a book.

Susan LOVES connecting with her fans!